"It's late," she said. "I should—"

She nodded toward the door of the second bedroom. She ran her tongue over her lower lip, then caught it between her teeth, the sensuous motion fixating his gaze there.

"You should," he agreed softly. He leaned to her, gently cupping her face, and brushed a kiss against her cheek, lingering long enough for it to become a caress of breath and lips on her skin. He wanted more, to love her until they were both boneless and breathless.

"Thank you."

"For what?"

"For not giving up on me."

Dear Reader,

Whether this is your first or a return visit to
Luna Hermosa, New Mexico, and the Garrett/Morente
families, we welcome you to our favorite fictional town.

Over the last five stories in THE BROTHERS OF
RANCHO PINTADA series, new bonds have been
forged and a family reunited. But there are still secrets
in patriarch Jed Garrett's past yet to be revealed that
none of the brothers, or even Jed himself, could have
expected.

From the beginning, we wanted to write a family
story about people with imperfect lives finding perfect
love, living in a town alive with things that matter to
us—community, friends and familiarity.

The Morentes, the Garretts and the women they love
have so many of the joys, passions, heartbreaks, hopes
and dreams we all have that we're happy we'll be there
with them to tell all their stories.

Nicole Foster

HEALING THE M.D.'S HEART

NICOLE FOSTER

SPECIAL EDITION®

Published by Silhouette Books

America's Publisher of Contemporary Romance

SILHOUETTE BOOKS

ISBN-13: 978-0-373-65448-2
ISBN-10:   0-373-65448-0

Recycling programs
for this product may
not exist in your area.

HEALING THE M.D.'S HEART

Visit Silhouette Books at www.eHarlequin.com

Printed in U.S.A.

Books by Nicole Foster

Silhouette Special Edition

Sawyer's Special Delivery #1703
The Rancher's Second Chance #1841
What Makes a Family? #1853
The Cowboy's Lady #1913
The Bridesmaid's Turn #1926
Healing the M.D.'s Heart #1966

Harlequin Historical

Jake's Angel #522
Cimarron Rose #560
Hallie's Hero #642

*The Brothers of Rancho Pintada

NICOLE FOSTER

is the pseudonym for the writing team of Danette Fertig-Thompson and Annette Chartier-Warren. Both journalists, they met while working on the same newspaper, and started writing historical romance together after discovering a shared love of the Old West and happy endings. Their seventeen-year friendship has endured writer's block, numerous caffeine-and-chocolate deadlines, and the joyous chaos of marriage and raising five children between them. They love to hear from readers. Send a SASE for a bookmark to PMB 228, 8816 Manchester Rd., Brentwood, MO 63144.

Chapter One

Nearly a thousand miles from home, Duran Forrester wanted to believe, after all the regretted decisions, frustrations and slams into brick walls over the last months, that this wasn't the biggest mistake of his life.

Then he reminded himself it didn't matter. Even if it was, there was no undoing it because he was fast running out of options. More importantly, he was running out of time.

He glanced in the rearview mirror at his son. Noah, his dark hair ruffled and cheeks flushed, sweat beading on his brow, slumped sideways on the seat asleep, clutching his scruffy stuffed panda in a one-armed hug. Ten minutes...ten minutes and they'd be in Luna Hermosa and he'd have Noah at a hospital.

It's only an ear infection. Some antibiotics and painkillers and he'll be okay. He'll be fine. He has to be.

He repeated it to himself as if it were a mantra that could shield him from the fear that struck at him with its cold, sharp edge of panic. And like all the other times, he wondered if this would be when he'd be told it wasn't okay, that his son would never be fine.

Noah shouldn't be here, that much now was obvious. Duran had a long debate with himself over whether or not to bring his son along in the first place. Noah had had enough disappointments in his life and Duran didn't want this trip to be one more. But once he'd found out Duran's destination, Noah had been so excited and after three days of his seven-year-old's persistent wheedling, begging and insisting, Duran finally gave in. Despite his misgivings, he'd convinced himself that the trip, if nothing else, would give him precious time with Noah, a few weeks uninterrupted by work and everything life had recently thrown at them.

They'd been less than an hour from their destination when things started to go wrong. Noah's temperature spiked, he'd started complaining about his ears hurting and Duran's reason fought his impulse to slam his foot on the accelerator and say to hell with speed limits.

He gripped the steering wheel hard enough to imprint the shape of his hands there, finding it a poor release for the turmoil of worry, frustration, uncertainty and anger that hit him in surges despite his best efforts to keep it shoved to a dark corner of his mind. Mostly everything—his and Noah's current predicament, the surprises of the past weeks that more often than not had been unwelcome—he could only blame on himself and his recently acquired determination to find out who'd he'd been before Eliza and Luke Forrester had made him their son.

He'd known, since he was younger than Noah, that he'd been adopted, but never had the least desire to find his birth parents until now. His adoptive parents were loving and generous people, devoted to each other and to him, who'd made him feel that it didn't matter why he'd been given away, only that they were blessed in choosing him and that with them was where he belonged.

The *why* still didn't matter; now and urgently, the *who* did. Looking at Noah again, he wished, for his son's sake, he had another choice. And he prayed, hard and long, this didn't turn out as badly as when he'd contacted the woman who considered him *her* biggest mistake. His birth mother.

I didn't want you then. There's nothing I can do for you now. It was a long time ago. My family doesn't know about you and I plan to keep it that way.

No amount of pleas or appeals changed her mind.

But she had given him something—two names and another chance to keep his hope alive.

The first he couldn't allow himself to think about right now.

It was my kind of luck, all bad. It wasn't anything but too much whiskey and one long night with that cowboy, and then he disappeared and I ended up with the two of you.

Two. And just that fast he found out he was a twin. Ry Kincaid hadn't wanted to be found and even less wanted to be called his brother. But neither of them could deny who they were and after an uneasy meeting, had left it unresolved while Duran made it his business to track down the second name on his list.

Jed Garrett. Rancho Piñtada, Luna Hermosa, New Mexico.

His father—and the man he wanted to meet most…and least.

The little girl grinned and Lia Kerrigan smiled back, returning an exuberant hug, accepting a kiss made slightly sticky by Nina's refusal to give up her sucker. Lia only wished these infrequent office visits didn't amount to the majority of time she got to spend with her youngest sister. Then again, for a woman with seven siblings, it was amazing how little time she'd spent with any of them. Her oldest brother she'd never even met, and the others were more like strangers with whom she happened to share a parent.

Old pain, made worse by the knowledge that as much as she cared for Nina, inevitably they would end up with the same distant relationship. Circumstance and the more than thirty years' difference in age would see to that.

Lia immediately pushed the maudlin thought away, putting it down to too many working hours at the hospital and her office and her dad showing up with Nina ten minutes before the much anticipated end of her eleven-hour day. It was typical of him and yet it never failed to irritate her. Walter Kerrigan was a successful orthopedic surgeon who should have understood better than anyone the demands on his daughter's time. But since the day Nina, his fifth child, was born, he'd insisted on making the drive from Santa Fe anytime he decided Nina needed to see a pediatrician, disregarding Lia's repeated requests for at least an advance phone call.

"Madelyn wants to know if you're planning to come to the housewarming," her father asked when Nina, locating the stack of books Lia kept in her examining room, was happily engrossed in studying her favorite. "She says she's left you several messages, but you haven't gotten back to her."

Lia stopped herself from sighing. Walter's fourth wife was twenty-nine to his sixty-two. In fact, Madelyn was six years younger than Lia herself, but the only thing they had in common was that they were both female. Lia couldn't think of a worse way to spend a Saturday night than a party at her dad's new house. It was impossible not to love Nina, but she couldn't say the same for Nina's mother. "I've been busy," she gave the usual excuse. "And I may be on call this weekend."

"You always say that," Walter said, his dismissive tone clearly saying he didn't believe her. "It wouldn't hurt if you would come to visit us once in a while, if nothing else to see Nina. You complain enough about not being able to spend time with her. Bring that fireman of yours—I can't remember his name—the one you've been seeing."

"Tonio Peña, and that's been over for more than a year now."

"Has it?" Walter assessed his daughter with the slight concentrated frown that he gave a particularly difficult-to-treat injury. "I suppose he went the way of the others. Relationships seem to be a self-fulfilling prophecy with you. You expect them to turn out badly and so they do."

"You taught me well," Lia retorted, defensiveness sharpening her voice more than she'd intended. Maybe there was some truth in what he said, but her father, who acquired and discarded wives and girlfriends as easily as if he were trading in a car for a better model, could hardly claim to be an expert on successful relationships.

"The difference between us is it doesn't hurt me when it falls apart," Walter said. "Unlike you, I gave up my illusions that anything lasts forever a long time ago. There are advantages to being married, but they aren't so great that I feel the need to sentence myself to a lifetime of misery if it doesn't work."

That apparently was one philosophy he and her mother shared, Lia reflected, after her father and Nina had left. Shaking off her unprofitable introspection—it certainly hadn't gotten her anywhere in the past—she finished the notations on Nina's chart and was seriously contemplating a long bath and a cold drink when her pager beeped. Bath and drink became unlikely when she recognized the number as the emergency room extension.

"Doctor Nunez wanted to know if you could help with a

sick case, a little boy," the nurse said when Lia called in. "We're busy this evening, and Doctor Nunez thought you could handle it more quickly."

Translation: Hector doesn't like kids. The thought of inflicting a harried Hector Nunez on a sick child was more than enough to hurry her to the emergency room.

Her first thought entering the curtained cubicle was the man sitting on the edge of the examining table, a protective arm around the boy curled up against his chest, was going to be difficult. His expression clearly said he was prepared to treat anyone who approached his son as an adversary until proven otherwise. Yet glancing over the boy's chart, she thought he'd probably earned the right.

The paperwork raised questions, though, about what Duran Forrester, who listed his profession as filmmaker and gave an address in Los Angeles, was doing a thousand miles from home, in Luna Hermosa of all places, with a sick child.

"Mr. Forrester?" She gave him a quick appraisal, getting a fast impression of unruly dark brown hair that tended to slant over one eye and a runner's body, long, hard and lean under the black shirt and jeans. The silver stud earring he wore and his sensual good looks probably had people mistaking him for someone who spent his time in front of the camera rather than behind it. His eyes, trained on her now, gave her the feeling he was sizing her up and that she so far hadn't measured up to his standards. She wasn't exactly at her best after nearly twelve long hours, her khaki slacks and white shirt showing the day's wear, makeup faded and her dark auburn hair doing its best to escape her ponytail. But there was nothing she could do to fix that now, and so she pulled her professionalism around her, put on a polite smile and settled for ignoring it.

"I'm Lia Kerrigan, I'm the staff pediatrician." As she came

around to the bedside opposite Duran Forrester, the boy half glanced at her, his eyes dull with fever. "You must be Noah. Or maybe this is Noah?" She tweaked the ear of the stuffed panda the boy clutched tightly.

A spark briefly flared in the boy's eyes. "That's Percy."

"Percy's a nice name for a puppy," Lia said conversationally as she started her exam, working around the bear and Duran Forrester, aware he was closely watching her every move.

"He's not a puppy," Noah protested. "He's a panda."

"Really?" Lia took a quick temperature reading while she gave the bear due consideration. "Are you sure?"

Noah held up his friend for inspection. "See?"

"Mmm...well, you could be right. But since I've never actually *seen* a real panda before, I'm not sure."

"I saw two, once. In a zoo. They were awesome." Noah leaned back against his dad's shoulder. "My ears hurt."

"I know, honey," Lia said softly, gently stroking a few wayward locks of hair from his forehead. Noah so much resembled his dad, a younger version of the man with the same messy dark hair and deep river-green eyes, that she could easily imagine Duran Forrester as a child. Illness, though, had paled Noah and painted violet shadows under his eyes. "I'm going to see what I can do to fix that."

Giving Noah what she hoped was a reassuring smile, she moved around the bed nearer to Duran. "Normally, I'd send him home with an antibiotic. But you two are a long way from home and Noah's circumstances require special care—" She let the sentence trail off, not sure how much she should say with Noah listening. "I think it would be better if he stayed the night. I'm sure you understand there could be complications and I could do a better job of monitoring him from here."

He didn't answer right away, but gave her that assessing

look, clearly weighing her advice against his own judgment. Lia thought it was even odds whether he'd agree to her suggestion. Finally, he gave a curt nod. "All right. If you think it's best."

"I don't wanna stay here," Noah said. "I wanna go home."

"Not tonight, buddy," Duran told him, putting his arm around Noah again and drawing him closer. "It's just one night. And I'll stay with you, I promise."

"Sure he will, and Percy, too," Lia added. "You're lucky he's not a puppy, though. We don't let puppies in here. But pandas are different. They get to be special guests."

Diverting Noah's attention from having to spend night in a hospital room, Lia made a big show of giving Percy his own ID bracelet, checking his heartbeat and finding him a surgical cap to keep his ears warm, earning her Noah's approval and most surprising, a smile from Duran Forrester. It wasn't much, a quick sideways slant of his mouth, but it warmed some of the cold places inside and left in their place a warm, satisfied glow.

She personally saw to settling Noah in a room, and after getting him to eat a little chicken noodle soup and drink some apple juice, she tucked him into bed. Drowsy from the mild painkillers she'd given him, his eyes drooped closed almost immediately, and Lia, straightening, looked directly into Duran's frown.

"I need to make a call," he said, fixing his attention on Noah. "I've missed an appointment I had here and I should let him know where I am." He patted his shirt pocket, came up empty, and his scowl deepened. "Damn, I left the number in the car."

Lia considered telling him she'd stay with Noah while he retrieved the number and made his call, but figured, as protective he was of his son, he wouldn't agree. "Where were you headed? This is a small enough town, I might be able to help you."

"Rancho Piñtada. I was supposed to meet with a Rafe Garrett at five."

Whatever she expected, it wasn't that. "Are you a rancher as well as a filmmaker?" she asked lightly, curious, but not wanting to probe.

"No. My business is personal." He didn't volunteer anything else and she heeded the clear message to back off.

"I know Rafe and Jule. I'm their pediatrician, too." She grabbed up a brochure from beside the bed and scrawled down the number. "Rafe should be at home by now, especially if you were supposed to meet with him." Hesitating, she reconsidered her unspoken offer and then said, "I'll sit with Noah while you make your call, if you like. I don't mind. Technically I'm off duty and there's nowhere else I need to be. And he shouldn't wake up in the few minutes it'll take to make your call."

Again, she got silence and that look and then finally, he unbent a little. "Thanks," he said gruffly. "I'll make it quick."

He pushed his way out of the room, leaving Lia to drop into the chair beside Noah's bed. She watched him as he slept, wondering at Duran Forrester, who he was and why he was here, what personal business he could have with Rafe. It was none of her business, but she couldn't help but be curious, partly because Rafe's family was famous for their dramas, but mostly because of the air of secrecy Duran insisted on keeping close around himself and his son. She recalled the paperwork and the deliberate empty space under mother's name, as if Noah's mother had never existed. Questions, and more questions, and she wasn't likely ever to get any answers.

Duran didn't leave her much time to speculate. He came back less than ten minutes later, his expression blanked, as if he'd gotten news that had blindsided him. Mindful of his emotional privacy, she pretended not to notice. "Were you able to reach Rafe?"

Nodding, he moved to stand by Noah, staring down at his son. Very gently, he brushed his fingertips over the sleeping boy's cheek. The love in his face was clear and strong, and yet there was grieving in it, too. Lia had to stop herself from reaching out to him, the desire to comfort was that powerful even though she knew any reassurance she could offer would be hollow and unwelcome, coming from a stranger.

For some reason—though she knew it what was she should do—she couldn't simply detach herself from the situation, walk away, go home and leave Duran Forrester to face the long night ahead, with only his fears for Noah as company. It wasn't her job to stay; she'd already done far more for the two of them than usual. Yet she had the impression, without having any real basis for knowing, that Duran was alone in more than just the sense of being a stranger in town and that kept her in the room, giving herself excuses to stay.

"I know Noah wasn't very hungry earlier," she ventured, a poor outlet for her feelings but the best she could do, "but you didn't get any dinner at all. How about I bring us both something? I don't know about you, but lunch was a long time ago for me."

"You don't have to do that."

"No, but you're alone in a strange town with a sick little boy and you're going to be spending the night in a very uncomfortable chair. The least I can do is treat you to some of our gourmet hospital cuisine. Besides, like I said, I'm hungry, too." Not giving him an opportunity to refuse, she got up and moved quickly to the door. "I'll be back."

Calling the cafeteria from the nurses' desk, she asked for the meals to be delivered to Noah's room. Then she checked in with the night staff and her service, telling them she was off duty but intended to stay for a while to monitor Noah. By the time she was done, the food had arrived and she slipped back inside the room. Duran had dimmed the lights and was sitting in the chair facing the bed, his forehead propped on his fist, weariness evident in the slump of his body.

"It's not the best," she said, indicating the trays when he glanced up, "but at least it's dinner."

He pushed himself up in the chair, nodded in reply and they ate in silence for a few minutes, the air in the room thick with things they left unsaid. Finally, he pushed the tray aside and, speaking quietly so as to not disturb Noah, asked, "Is everyone in town as nice as you?"

She laughed, inexplicably self-conscious at his compliment. "I don't think I can answer that without sounding as if I'm bragging or dissing someone else. There are a lot of good people here. It's why I've stayed for so long. I like being in a smaller town. I'm sure it's considerably different from L.A., though," she added, risking a comment on his personal life, even if it was of the most innocuous kind.

"Night and day," he agreed, seeming not to mind. "But I've only lived there since college. I grew up not far from here, just outside Rio Rancho. This is not that different." Leaning back, he tilted his head against the wall, briefly closing his eyes. "I'm thinking about moving back, at least to New Mexico— work permitting, that is. I've arranged things so I'm between projects and I can have some time to decide. But, ultimately, L.A. isn't the best place to raise a child."

"I can only imagine living in a place like L.A. Even so, you seem to have done a good job with Noah. I know it's not easy raising a child on your own."

"Personal experience?"

"Hardly," she said, the laugh this time sounding more like a harsh exclamation. "But I am a pediatrician. I see lots of different kinds of families."

He raised his head to look at her, with that intense, disconcerting way of his that gave her the sensation he was dissecting her soul. "I always wanted the same kind of family I had growing up for Noah. I really did have the two great parents, the faithful dog and the New Mexico version of a white picket fence."

"But?"

"But my ex-wife didn't see it that way. She walked out before Noah turned one, got a quick divorce, gave me full custody and I haven't seen her since. So Noah's had to get by with just me."

"He doesn't appear to have suffered for it," Lia said softly. "And things could change."

"Not for me," he said in a tone that put a full stop to any ideas he would ever contemplate another serious relationship. "I won't risk putting Noah through that, loving someone and then losing them. He's been through enough already. He was too young when his mother left to realize she didn't want him. He sometimes asked why he doesn't have a mother and I still don't know what to tell him."

She could understand and yet there was sadness in the finality of his words, his certainty that love would never touch his life again with enough strength to make him want to take another chance. But then again, didn't she, better than anyone, know that the odds were he was right, that it was as likely to turn out badly as well? Any parent who loved his child as much as he did would consider the risks not worth it—unlike her own parents, to whom children were apparently incidental to disposable relationships.

A light knock on the door interrupted them and Lia, thinking it was the night nurse, got up to answer it. Instead, she found herself face-to-face with Cort Morente, a friend, but one of the last people she would have guessed she'd be seeing here and tonight.

"Cort—how did you know…?" She stared at him, completely confused. Duran had said he was in Luna Hermosa to meet with Rafe and now Rafe's younger brother showed up here, out of the blue. "Is something wrong with one of the kids?" she asked, although she couldn't imagine why Cort wouldn't have just called her if there was a problem with one of his four children, even if it had been an emergency.

"No, they're all fine. I wasn't looking for you." Cort looked behind her to where Duran had gotten to his feet and Lia instinctively stepped aside. The two men faced each other, Duran tense, already on the defensive, and Cort cautious, as if weighing his options before making a move. When he finally did, it easily qualified as something she'd never expected him to say.

"I came to see my brother."

Duran's first reaction was the completely irrelevant thought that maybe meeting unknown relations got easier after the first one. If so, by the time he'd gotten through all the relatives he seemed to have acquired, it should be simple, no struggling with mixed feelings or debating whether he was doing the right thing for Noah and himself.

Rafe Garrett had at least warned him, when Duran had called to postpone their meeting, that he and Ry Kincaid weren't Duran's only brothers. Five of Jed Garrett's sons were living in Luna Hermosa and for some reason Rafe didn't make clear, none of them wanted him to meet Jed first. He supposed this one had been elected to come here and determine what exactly it was that Duran wanted. From the steady, calculating gaze he got, Duran guessed Cort Morente's business depended on him being a quick and accurate judge of character and that Cort was deciding the truth of his claim to being Jed's son and what his motives were for showing up in Luna Hermosa.

Duran glanced back at Noah. His son slept on soundly, oblivious to the drama around him. Leaving Noah's bedside wasn't Duran's first choice, but Noah would likely be asleep for hours yet and he didn't want this first meeting with his Luna Hermosa relations constrained by the need for quiet and the concern Noah might wake up and overhear.

Lia must have sensed his hesitation because she took a step closer to the bed and told him, "I'll stay with him."

The rush of gratitude at her understanding seemed too intense, out of place for her simple gesture. But for an odd moment, Duran felt they were allies.

"If you wouldn't mind—" he flicked a hand toward the door "—I think you could help explain. You understand…"

Without a pause, she nodded and after checking Noah once more, followed him and Cort outside the room.

Duran turned to Cort, not sure where to start.

Cort spoke up first. "This is not how we intended this meeting to happen. But when Rafe called and told us about your son, we wanted to see if there was anything we could do." He made the offer and it sounded sincere. But there was a certain reservation in his manner—not quite suspicion, but a withholding of trust, an unwillingness to take Duran's claim of kinship at face value.

He couldn't blame the man; he hadn't brought any proof of his blood tie to Jed Garrett. He had none for himself, except the word of the stranger who had given birth to him. But he had to convince Cort Morente to make good on that offer because he couldn't afford to fail the way he had with his birth mother.

"Don't take this wrong, but I'm finding it hard right now to get my head around going from being an only child to having six brothers," Duran said slowly. "To be honest, though, it's more than I could have hoped for under the circumstances, especially if you meant it when you said you wanted to help."

"Mr. Forrester—" Lia began. "Duran," she amended when he looked at her. "If it makes it any easier—" She stopped, and he could see in her eyes she wanted to intervene, maybe spare him having to say it, but knew it was his to tell.

"I'm not trying to make it harder," Cort said, "but I can't say I'm not curious about those circumstances. Jed doesn't know you and your brother exist or, believe me, the rest of us would have heard about it by now. I have to wonder why you decided to track him down after all this time."

"I never knew he existed, either. My—" he couldn't call the woman his mother "—she didn't put his name on my birth certificate. I had to find her first to get it."

"Are you sure Jed's your father then?"

"She is. She gave me his name and the name of his ranch and the town it was in. It's all she gave me," he added, unable to keep the anger that still lingered from his meeting with the woman out of his voice, "except to tell me about Ry—Ry Kincaid, my twin. I didn't know about him until a few weeks ago. We were split up after we were born." Drawing in a long breath, he tried to let it out slowly, to ease some of the tension crawling up his back and neck, stiffening his muscles. "I never cared about whether or not I had any other relatives, it didn't matter."

Cort assessed him and Duran understood that Cort, too,

was protecting someone—his brothers, his family, maybe even Jed Garrett. "And it matters now," Cort said flatly, a statement of fact rather than a question.

"More than anything. I've been trying to track down as many blood relatives as I can. I'm running out of time." He steeled himself to say what he hadn't dared acknowledge in his head, yet battled daily in his nightmares. "My son is dying."

Chapter Two

He'd succeeded in shaking Cort's composure and it brought a surge of what almost felt like triumph because he knew, without having any basis for his certainty except gut instinct, that this time, he wouldn't be turned away.

"I'm sorry," Cort said, a husky note in his voice replacing his earlier coolness. "I've got four kids and I can't imagine..." He scrubbed a hand over his face and when he looked back this time the sympathy in his eyes was clear. "There has to be something we can do to help or you wouldn't be here."

"There is. Noah needs a bone marrow transplant, but they haven't been able to find a match."

"Noah has a rare immune-system illness," Lia explained for him. "There's been a lot of success in treating it with bone marrow transplants. But without it—" She looked at Duran, an apology in her eyes. "Without it, the prognosis isn't good. Noah probably won't survive past his late teens. The sooner he gets a transplant, the better his chances, and the odds of finding a match among blood relations are much higher."

"Which is why I went searching for my birth parents when neither I, my ex-wife nor any of her family turned out to be a match," Duran added. "I was hoping one of my birth parents would be a match, or if not, that maybe I had other relatives that would be. That's why I said discovering I had five brothers here is a better outcome than I could have wished for."

Cort nodded. "Then neither your twin nor your birth mother was a match, either."

"Ry wasn't. The only thing the tests proved was that we were brothers. And she refused to be tested." Anger flared up in him again and he pushed it down. There was nothing he could do to change the past or her mind and it wouldn't aid his appeal now. "She said she didn't want her family to know how badly she'd screwed up over thirty years ago. According to her, admitting to having sex once when she was twenty-two with a stranger she'd met in a bar would ruin her life."

"Jed won't give a damn. His family already knows the worst of his sins and a one-night stand hardly ranks." Cort hesitated and Duran readied himself for another disappointment. "He's sick though, dying. He couldn't be a donor even if he wanted to be. But I'm sure I can speak for my brothers and say we'd all be willing to be tested as soon as you can arrange it." He turned to Lia. "Is there anything you can do to expedite things?"

"I'll do whatever I can," she assured him. "I can't get anything done over the weekend, but I'll see what I can do about setting things up for early next week."

Duran found himself holding his breath, waiting to be told it was a mistake; that it wasn't going to happen the way he wanted. When that didn't come the sense of relief hit him hard, as if all the air had left the room and rushed back, and with it, a little of his faith in the future.

He searched for words to convey his feelings, but the thankfulness he felt was so tangled up with other, less defined and more uneasy emotions connected with finding brothers, a twin, discovering parts of himself he never knew—emotions that he hadn't given himself time to process—that it left him floundering for what to say to the stranger who could end up saving his son's life.

But Cort spared him from having to say anything by moving the conversation to practicalities. "I'm guessing you're staying the night here with Noah. But when he gets out of the hospital, you and he can stay with one of us." He forestalled any protest Duran would have made by holding up a hand. "A hotel's no place for a sick kid. The ranch would be best. There's plenty of room at the big house and Rafe and Josh are only a few minutes away. But that means telling Jed, and soon." He pinched the bridge of his nose, wincing. "I don't see any way around it."

"I get the feeling he's not going to be happy to find out he has two more sons," Duran said. If that was the case, he was glad that Jed Garrett had sons who, if not happy to learn of his existence, were at least willing to accept him as a brother and do what they could for Noah.

"No, it'll probably be just the opposite," Cort said grimly. Apparently he saw Duran was starting to get frustrated with the veiled hints about Jed's character and offered a rueful smile. "Sorry, I'm not deliberately trying to keep you in the dark. But it's going to take some time to explain and I'd rather not do it here."

"Later then, or not," he said. "My concern right now is Noah."

"I understand. Why don't you give me or Rafe a call

tomorrow, when you figure out what's going on with Noah and one of us can run by and help you two get settled somewhere else?"

"About that—" Duran began. He felt uncomfortable accepting hospitality from strangers, even if he was related to them.

It was Lia who resolved the matter for him. "Say yes. Otherwise I'll have to call security because Cort never takes no for an answer and that's the only other way we'll get rid of him."

"Thanks for the character reference," Cort retorted.

"Thanks for the warning," Duran muttered and both Cort and Lia laughed, drawing a reluctant smile from him. "Fine, leave me a number and I'll let you know when Noah's released."

Cort handed over a cell and home number and as it seemed to finish anything else they could say for now, an awkward silence intruded.

With a shift of his shoulders that telegraphed their shared uncertainty about where they should take this next, Cort finally spoke. "I should be going. You need to get back to your son and I need to get home to my family. I'll talk to you, both of you—" he glanced at Lia "—soon."

Duran waited until he'd gone and then by tacit agreement, he and Lia went back inside the room to check on Noah. He stood to one side while she bent over his sleeping son, not liking her frown when she finished taking his temperature again.

"It hasn't come down much," she said in answer to his pointed look. "We'll monitor it for the next several hours, and if it doesn't improve, then I'm going to start him on intravenous antibiotics. He may have had those before, if he's had other infections."

His eyes on Noah, Duran nodded. More hospital time, more treatments that would only buy a temporary respite, not the permanent answer Noah needed. "I should never have brought him along."

"It wouldn't have made any difference. The infection's been going on for a couple of days, at least, probably since before you left L.A., and it would have been worse for him if he'd been sick while you were gone. At least here you and Noah are together and you've got—" she looked lost for an appropriate word, settling on "—family you can rely on to help."

"I'm not quite ready to consider them family and whether or not I can rely on them remains to be seen."

"You can—rely on them, I mean. I've known four of them for years, and they're all good guys."

He noticed she deliberately avoided referring to them as his brothers, perhaps because of his comment wary of acknowledging a blood link between him and the others. "You don't seem surprised to find out Garrett's got two more sons."

"Not really," she said. "Jed's five sons here were by four different women, and the oldest one he didn't even acknowledge until a few months ago. I'd have been more surprised if it had turned out the five of them were the only children he fathered."

Duran shook his head, not yet ready to learn any more about what was obviously a convoluted family tree. "Noah wants to meet them all. When I explained to him why I was coming here, that I had found out I had more family than just his grandparents, that's all he could talk about." He lightly stroked his hand over his son's tousled hair. "He's lonely, with just him and me, and because he's been sick for so long. My ex-wife's family decided that he and I didn't exist after Amber left me. So the idea of having more family is exciting—to him. But he doesn't have to think about the consequences."

"That one of them might not be a match?"

"That they might not care about knowing him, or that it's all temporary. We stay here for a while and then he never sees them again."

Suddenly, Duran felt tired, drained by the emotional roller-coaster ride he'd been on for what seemed like years now. He heard himself, a damning echo in his head, admitting Noah was dying and all the fear, grief and worry he'd been shouldering alone for so many months welled up in him, tearing at his control.

Turning away from the sympathy in Lia's eyes, he leaned his hands on the back of a chair, head bowed, struggling to regain his composure. There was a pause, a whisper of sound and then a gentle hand touched his shoulder.

"You're doing everything you can," she said softly.

"It hasn't been enough so far, what if it isn't enough now?"

"Then you keep trying. Because even if it isn't enough, that's all you can do."

If it wasn't enough, it would break him. There would be no compromises with his emotions, no comfort in telling himself he'd done his best. "I can't let that happen," he said, but instead of coming out as clear, hard resolve, it sounded desperate, already cracked with sorrow.

"Duran—" Lia reached around and laid her hand against his jaw, turning him to face her. Whatever she saw in his expression prompted her to abandon what she intended to say and before he understood, he was in her arms, she was holding him or he was holding her, and it didn't matter because it had been so long since he shared the burden, that giving even a little of it up, for however short a time, was like being able to breathe again.

The moment stretched into many, into time he couldn't measure, before the comfort she offered and he grasped at became too much to accept and he very carefully pulled out of her embrace. Still within touching distance, they stood looking at each other and for the first time, he saw her as a woman and not the doctor who'd stepped in to help a stranger in need. She was barely to his shoulder, on the thin side of slender, and there was a delicacy about her, as if she were finely made and vulnerable to the rigors of life. Her dark red hair was gilded with copper and gold in the dim light, her eyes an unusual shade of light brown. He might have, at first glance, dismissed her as merely decorative, with little substance, except he had felt the strength in her hands, seen the intelligence and empathy in her eyes, been touched by her warmth even when he thought himself immune.

She accepted his study for a minute or two and then dropped her eyes and took an uncertain step back. "I'm sorry. I shouldn't have—"

"Don't be." Duran resisted the urge to reach out to her, to reassure her that she'd misinterpreted his moving away from her; he'd been alone for so long it had become habit to throw up his defenses when he was most vulnerable. "I appreciate everything you've done so far. You've gone way out of your way to help us."

"Yes, well, that is my job," she said briskly. She avoided eye contact with him and busied herself taking Noah's temperature again. "I'll have the nurse check him again in a couple of hours. If there's no change, then we'll start the IV. But we'll keep our fingers crossed he won't need it this time. I'll be back first thing in the morning, unless there's a problem before then."

For some reason, her determined return to professional detachment irritated him. It felt jarringly out of place, though by all rights, it shouldn't have. "Does this mean I have to start calling you Dr. Kerrigan again?"

"You haven't called me anything," she said. A slight smile touched her mouth, bringing back a whisper of the warmth. "At least out loud."

"Okay, Lia," he said deliberately. "Then we'll see you in the morning."

This time the smile blossomed. "Count on it."

Lia left the hospital, her body tired, but thoughts and emotions too unsettled to let her rest. It was late, nearly ten, but the notion of going home and confessing her sins to her elderly cat didn't appeal. Instead, she decided to stop by Morente's and see if Nova could spare half an hour for a glass of wine.

She and Nova Vargas—six months now Mrs. Alex Tréjos—had been friends for a decade, ever since Lia had come to Luna Hermosa as a young intern and decided to make it home. Nova had been waitressing at the local diner—they'd met the first time Lia, new in town, came in search of a serious caffeine transfusion—and almost from the first they'd started a ritual, Lia sticking around after the diner closed, the two of them having coffee or a drink, sharing grievances and confidences. Since last year, when Nova had taken over managing the upscale Morente's and then in February, had married the local middle-school principal, they'd had less time together. But they both resolved to keep their weekly ritual, even if it meant an hour in Nova's office, sharing a margarita and whatever chocolate dessert was left over from the kitchen.

"Hey, girl, I didn't expect to see you here tonight," Nova greeted her with a hug before stepping back to give Lia a critical once-over. "I thought you were going to go home and actually relax for once."

"I was, but something came up."

"I hope he was tall, dark and gorgeous."

"He is, but he comes packaged with a short, dark and cute one," Lia said, smiling when Nova's mouth pulled up in an expression of serious disbelief. "I promise to tell all, if you've got time for a glass of wine."

"I can make time for this," Nova said and gestured Lia to follow her to the back office.

A few minutes later, settled on the office couch with a glass of wine and a generous serving of wickedly rich chocolate soufflé, Lia told her about Duran and his reason for coming to town to find Jed. She knew Nova wouldn't gossip. She was Cort's former lover and had married his best friend, and the three of them had stayed close. Besides, news got around fast enough in Luna Hermosa without Nova's help. Lia gave it less than a week before everyone would be talking about it.

Nova, like her, shrugged off the revelation of Jed fathering two more sons. "Everyone knows Jed Garrett likes women and lots of them. So what's this Duran Forrester like?"

"Tall, dark and gorgeous," Lia said lightly. She felt herself coloring and reached for another bite of soufflé to cover it, hoping Nova wouldn't notice. Bad enough she'd practically thrown herself into his arms back in Noah's room. She didn't need Nova deciding there was more going on than just her normal concern for the father of a seriously sick child.

"And?" Nova prompted.

"And he's a single father who loves his son and would make a deal with the devil to save his life."

"Ah." Taking a sip of her wine, Nova studied her for a moment. "You seem to have gone above and beyond to help him out."

"It's my job." Lia repeated the same excuse she'd given Duran.

"And you're doing it very thoroughly."

"It's not like that at all."

"Sure it isn't."

"Oh, for pity's sake, we spent most of our time together in a hospital room with his sick child. What could possibly have happened?"

"I don't know, you tell me," Nova said and Lia wanted to answer, *nothing, absolutely nothing,* except it felt like a lie. "I can imagine it'd be pretty easy to get attached to a sick little boy and a devoted single dad who came to a town full of strangers looking for someone to help save his son's life. And if he's as hot as you say he is—"

"I didn't say that," Lia protested.

"You didn't have to. Just be careful, okay? I know you want to help, but I also know how you are when it comes to getting too involved."

Her friend probably did, but Lia didn't want to be reminded of it right now. "And how am I?" she asked, knowing Nova would tell her if even if she didn't.

"I love you, but you have this way of sabotaging every relationship you're in because you're afraid it might work," Nova said.

"Oh, please, that's not true. And a few hours with a stranger hardly qualifies as a relationship."

"Look what happened with Tonio," Nova continued. "He started to get serious and you decided you were too busy to spend time with him. You kept pushing him away until he finally got fed up and left you. He and Rita Pérez are dating," she added, mentioning the name of one of Morente's waitresses. "In case you're interested."

It was hard, coming up with a defense, when Lia suspected—no, she knew—that Nova was probably right. "I'm not," she grumbled. "And you aren't exactly a model for a successful relationship, you know."

Nova laughed. "Until Alex, I never wanted one. My dad walking out on Mama and me cured me of wanting to tie myself to anyone for too long."

"You and Cort were together for years," Lia pointed out.

"Cort and I were lovers but we were never together. We were always just friends. Good friends," she added at Lia's skeptical look. "I liked being with him and he's one helluva lover. But, trust me, neither of us ever had the least intention of making it permanent."

"And now you're married," Lia said, emphasizing the word. "That can be pretty permanent."

"Can be? There speaks the cynic. I intend for it to be, honey."

"You can't know that," Lia said. She thought about everyone she'd ever loved and how, in one way or another, they'd all left her. Sometimes it had been a deliberate decision on their part; sometimes the fault could be assigned elsewhere, but the end result had been the same. "Things change, people go away."

Her dark eyes speaking her understanding, Nova said quietly, "Not always."

Maybe it worked for other people, but not for her. Lia had had hard lessons in loving and losing, ones she didn't intend to repeat. "Don't worry," she told Nova. "I don't plan on letting myself get involved beyond doing what I can for his son. That *is* my job."

"No, honey, that's the problem," Nova said. She tipped her wineglass toward Lia. "You don't ever plan on getting involved but you do. And then it's too late."

Not this time. It's not too late because nothing has started. And I won't let it.

She kept that thought with her long after she left the restaurant and took it home and to bed with her, using it as a shield against any doubts that crept in, any whispered warnings that she'd already started something she couldn't stop or turn back from, that it already was too late.

Chapter Three

The next morning, Lia edged open the door a few inches and looked into the still darkened hospital room, uncertain of her reception despite it being almost seven-thirty. Both still sleeping, neither son nor father knew she was there. She stood in the doorway for a moment simply watching them.

That Duran was sleeping at all surprised her. She couldn't imagine he was anything approaching comfortable. Awkwardly sitting at his son's side, he was bent halfway across the bed, one arm crooked under his head for a makeshift pillow, the other stretched out over the blanket to cradle Noah's small hand in his palm.

His position suggested he couldn't bear to be even a chair's length from his son and an odd feeling, both warmth and chill, twisted in her chest. She could imagine the fear and uncertainty Duran lived with constantly; his desperation in trying to hold on to the little person who meant everything to him. It wasn't with the same intensity, but she, also, under-stood only too well the fear of losing someone you loved. For Duran—alone save for Noah—that fear at times had to be overwhelming.

Figuring Duran's night had been too short, she hesitated stepping any further inside, torn between not wanting to disturb him and needing to check on Noah. Concern for Noah won out. Quietly as possible, she moved close to the bed and gently brushed her fingers to Noah's cheek, pleased to find his skin cool and dry. The light touch made him wriggle and scrunch up his face as he blinked awake.

"Dr. Kerrigan?"

"That's right," Lia said barely above a whisper, giving him a reassuring smile. "I just came to check on you and Percy." She patted the panda's furry head. "Percy looks pretty good. How do you feel?"

"Okay, I guess." Noah thought for a moment, then added, "Hungry."

Lia laughed softly. "I think I can fix that. But I need to check your ears and take your temperature first. Then we'll see about getting you and your dad some breakfast."

"Why is Dad still sleeping?" Noah asked, frowning as he looked at his father. "He never sleeps late." Before Lia could intervene, he pushed at Duran's arm. "Dad—Dad, Dr. Kerrigan is here."

Duran stirred and sat up, looking at once disoriented and impossibly sexy. His dark, sleep-mussed hair fell over his brow. He yawned, stretched and with no more than a quick glance Lia's way, turned full attention to his son.

"Hey, good morning," he said, smiling as he smoothed Noah's hair back from his forehead. "You look like you're feeling a lot better."

"I woke up before you."

"I see that. Guess I was being lazy today."

Noah giggled at that and Lia couldn't help but smile. She scarcely knew him, but what she had learned of Duran Forrester made for an attractive package: fiercely loving, responsible father, effortlessly sexy guy, a man not easily deterred once he'd chosen a course of action. And—and she needed to stop where this was going because it was so far off course from where her focus should be.

As though he sensed her eyes on him, Duran looked up, giving her half a smile. "Sorry, I didn't fall asleep until nearly six. You were right about the uncomfortable chair."

"No, I'm sorry. I didn't mean to wake you. I just needed to check on Noah."

Duran stood up, walking stiffly at first, taking a few paces around the room as Lia bent over Noah, satisfying herself that the antibiotics and fever reducers had done their job. Noah's temperature was normal again and although it would be a few days before the infection cleared, his ears didn't seem as painful for him as the night before.

Finishing, she briefly squeezed the boy's shoulder. "Okay, I think we'll let you and Percy out of here in a little bit—after breakfast," she added at his hopeful look. "Give me a few minutes and I'll see what I can rustle up."

"You don't have to do that," Duran started.

"I promised," Lia said, winking at Noah as she headed for the door.

She returned fifteen minutes later, backing into the room, balancing the heavy tray.

"Whatever that is it smells great," Duran said, relieving her of her load.

"Nothing too fancy, I'm afraid, but at least the coffee's

decent. And it's a definite improvement over the oatmeal they'd be bringing you, Noah. Unless you like your oatmeal kinda gray and sticky?" Noah made a face and Lia laughed. "I didn't think so. How about some eggs and bagels instead?"

"I think you've just saved my life." Duran, accepting a mug of coffee, breathed an appreciative sigh over the hot brew as Noah dug into his breakfast. "I can go without just about anything—"

"—except decent coffee," Lia chimed in and they finished the sentence in unison.

"An addict after my own heart, I see."

"With the hours I keep, believe me, it's survival."

Duran smiled, for the first time giving her a full, open gesture of appreciation, unrestrained by reluctance or circumstance. A subtle, insidious heat curled through her, and she cursed it, irritated at herself for being so susceptible to a simple smile that didn't mean anything except his gratitude for a cup of coffee and her sparing his son overcooked oatmeal.

"Thank you again," he said, "for everything. You've made this whole ordeal a lot easier. Right, guy?" He glanced at Noah.

Noah, in the process of stuffing a chunk of bagel in his mouth, nodded. "I hate hospitals," he mumbled around the bread. "But you made it not so bad."

Whatever she could have said stuck in her throat and left her swallowing hard in blank silence. Looking at the trusting smile on Noah's pale face and the dark hollows shadowing his father's soulful eyes, she realized father and son had touched her in a way that would leave her marked, this time unable to maintain the detachment necessary to her job—to help them, then move on and forget.

It made no sense. She'd had many patients with serious, even terminal illnesses, but she'd always been able to distance herself enough to remain emotionally protected. She couldn't very well get deeply involved with the children she'd devoted her life to helping, to care too much, or she wouldn't be able to function as a professional. She'd learned that lesson well enough over the years. Until Duran Forrester and his little boy showed up, she'd stuck by it religiously.

Why were they different? Why did she feel this connection to them, this urgent need to do anything, *everything* to help? She had no answers.

"You're not having any?" Duran asked, jerking her out of her thoughts.

"What? Oh, no, thanks. I'm fine." She made herself focus on the business at hand. "There are a few things we should talk about, though. I did some checking and the earliest we can start the testing is Tuesday." Hesitating over whether or not she should bring up what was probably a touchy subject, she gave in to her need for answers and asked, "Were you planning on calling Cort this morning?"

"Calling him, yes." Duran pushed his coffee mug onto the tray and got to his feet. "Accepting his offer of housing—that I'm rethinking. I appreciate it, but I'm not comfortable with accepting it."

"Last night—"

"Last night I promised to call him. I didn't say I'd move in with any of them."

"They're family."

"No, they're strangers whom I happen to be related to. And I need some place quiet and stable—". He glanced at Noah. "I can better control that in a hotel."

"I could argue that," Lia persisted. Maybe she didn't have a right to interfere, but she knew Duran's brothers and their families, and she couldn't believe that they wouldn't accept

Noah as one of their own. In her opinion, that was better medicine right now than any other treatment she could prescribe. "A hotel is impersonal and there aren't any guarantees you're going to get the peace and quiet you want. Apart from that, weren't you the one who said—"

"I want to meet your family!" Noah broke in. "You said I had cousins."

Lia gestured to Noah, who'd made her point for her. "They aren't going to get the chance to know him if they never get to meet him."

His hardened expression clearly said Duran didn't like where the conversation was headed. For Noah's sake, though, Lia refused to back down. It might do Duran some good, as well, she reasoned. He'd been shouldering the weight of his son's illness alone. Support from any quarter had to be better for him than the isolation he'd imposed on himself. She assured herself she was doing the right thing because of Noah, ignoring the little nagging voice at the back of her head that she was far overstepping her boundaries, that she was involving herself in Duran's life far more than she should.

"I didn't come here for a family reunion," Duran said tightly.

"Didn't you? I thought that was the point."

"Why are you pushing this? Why is it so important to you?"

She could have answered that in ways that were personal, knowing in part she was letting her feelings about her own family and the distance she'd always felt between them influence her urging Duran to connect with his brothers. "It's important to you and to Noah," she answered instead and that was true, too. "Isn't it why you're here?"

Noah, oblivious to the tension, asked, "Are cousins like brothers and sisters?"

"Kind of," Duran answered, his attention on Lia momentarily diverted. "But cousins don't usually live in the same house as you, like brothers and sisters would."

"They can be especially good friends, though, because they're friends and they're family," Lia tried to explain, which was difficult, because for her it was only theory.

"I want to meet them," Noah insisted again, his mouth pulled in a stubborn line as he looked at his father. "You said I could."

"I know I did. But—" Duran pushed a hand through his hair and blew out a breath. "It's not that simple."

"Why?" Noah demanded.

Duran's frown accused Lia of pursuing a subject he'd wanted to avoid for as long as possible. "For a lot of reasons." He stopped, seemed to consider for a minute, then finally came to a decision. "I promised you'd meet them and you will. But it might not be right away and I don't know if staying in the same house with them is a good idea right now." This last was aimed at Lia and she flushed, knowing she probably deserved the reprimand but was unwilling to back down.

Before she could come back with a defense, the door pushed open and they were confronted with the morning nurse, followed by Cort.

Duran's eyes snapped to her, but Lia shook her head in denial she'd had anything to do with Cort's appearance.

"It's not her fault," Cort answered Duran's unspoken question. "I invited myself."

"Thinks he doesn't have to follow the rules like everyone else," the nurse grumbled. Toting a breakfast tray that was about as wide as she was, the nurse took one look at the stack of empty dishes on the table beside Noah and scowled at Lia. "I see someone's already done my job."

Lia hustled to explain. "I got here early and—"

"Oh, save it. I'll take the oatmeal home for Cruiser. Don't know what that dog sees in mushy oatmeal, but he gets plenty of it." She flung an accusatory look at Lia. "I suppose you've taken the boy's vitals, too?"

"I did, earlier, but I'm going to release him soon, so if you wouldn't mind checking them again, I'll have a quick word with Mr. Forrester and Cort outside."

"Fine, let me earn my keep, then. You three give me some space."

Heeding the older woman, Lia gestured Duran and Cort toward the door. "We'll just be a few minutes," she reassured Noah, who was eyeing the nurse doubtfully. "Don't worry, she's only cranky with adults."

"Forty years and I still get no respect," the sassy, rotund nurse muttered as the others left the room.

"Is she—?" Duran nodded to the door.

"No worries," Lia said. "She's the best pediatric nurse we have. She just saves her bedside manner for the kids."

Duran didn't seem convinced but looked to Cort. "I would have called."

"I'm sure you would have," Cort said easily. "But I figured it would be harder for you to turn down my offer in person. This way you can't hang up on me. So before you give me all the reasons why it won't work, I'll tell you that we've fixed it so you and Noah can stay at the ranch. My brother Josh used to live in one wing of the house. It's three rooms and more than big enough for the two of you."

"I don't doubt it," Duran said. "But this is all happening pretty fast. I'm not sure it's the best place for Noah right now."

"Trust me, the place is huge. You won't have to see Jed or Del—my stepmother—if you don't want to. Jed doesn't get around much these days, and Del—" Cort grimaced at his mention of Jed Garrett's wife. "Well, let's just say she'll be more than happy to stay out of your way."

"Noah would probably love being around all the animals," Lia put in.

Flicking a look at her, Duran said nothing for a moment. "You told Jed about me—us?"

For the first time, Cort looked uneasy. "Yeah, I told him everything. The timing wasn't ideal. He's been in Albuquerque for the past few days, seeing some specialist and won't be back until late this afternoon, so I had to do it by phone. But he knows."

"And?"

"And it was a shock. But like I predicted last night, once he got past the surprise, he was more than ready to bring two more sons into the family fold."

Cort's words and the troubled thread in his voice eroded Lia's previous confidence that staying at the ranch would be best for Duran and Noah. She'd been thinking of his brothers, instead of remembering who their father was. Jed Garrett might be sick, but it hadn't softened him, hadn't, as far as she could tell, caused him to repent his life of taking what he wanted, discarding anything and anyone that had stood in his way of building Rancho Piñtada into one of the biggest and most successful ranch operations in New Mexico. That had included wives, lovers and his own sons, and it was only recently that there had been a tentative attempt on his part to reconcile with the family he'd had no use for.

Duran, though, seemed strong enough in his resolve to save his son to face down any challenge without blinking, even the devil in the form of his newfound father. She'd no doubt that although it might be an awkward and even contentious first meeting, he'd be more than a match for Jed.

"What do you think?" Cort asked her pointedly.

Not liking him putting her on the spot, especially when she was already at odds with Duran over this, Lia forced an even tone. "I think the decision is up to Duran."

She thought she saw a flash of surprised gratitude in Duran's eyes, replaced quickly by a conflicted hesitation. "It's not that I don't appreciate this—"

"I understand," Cort said. "We all do, in one way or another. But you don't know how long you'll be here. Do you really want Noah living in a hotel for a month or more? Give it a night or two. If it doesn't work, then we'll figure out something that will."

"You know why I'm here," Duran reminded him. "If staying at the ranch doesn't work out—"

"Then it doesn't work out. It doesn't have anything to do with helping Noah."

"That's all any of us want," Lia couldn't help adding. She didn't know what to say that would convince Duran of his brothers' sincerity. There wasn't an easy way to describe the family the five of them had become despite the sins of their father that had nearly broken them apart forever.

She admired them, Sawyer, Rafe, Cort, Josh and Cruz. Somehow, against the odds and despite Jed, they had reconciled and become a true family. Lia envied them that, the bond they had.

And yet it would be tested once again, in a way none of them had expected. There were two more Garrett brothers now, strangers both, and one with a desperate need to find the person who could save his son's life.

Yet the fierce resolve in Cort's eyes answered the question of whether he and the others would stand together to help. "When you release Noah, they're coming back to the ranch with me," he said, leaving no room for argument. "You want to come along and help them get settled? You'd be best at explaining all the details of Noah's illness and what we need to do for the testing. Laurel and the kids are going to be there, too. We thought they'd be company for Noah."

Lia glanced at Duran, searching for a clue that he wanted her. He looked steadily back, seemingly searching himself before giving a brief nod. "Okay then, I'll get the paperwork started. If you're sure?" she asked him, still uncertain if he'd actually agreed to Cort's plan.

"I'm not sure," he said flatly. "But I'm not being given much of a choice."

"Then don't go."

"No." He shifted his gaze between her and Cort. "I'm going to give it a try, mostly because I promised Noah and I'm not going to go back on that." Turning, his hand on the door, he started back to his son, and over his shoulder, without looking at either of them, said, "I just hope I'm not going to regret it."

Five minutes after walking into the great room of Rancho Piñtada, Duran discovered the drawback to being raised an only child—being completely unprepared for the chaos and noise of a large family.

It was more than he'd hoped for. But it was also more than he'd anticipated, to the point that the combination of stress, lack of sleep, and being introduced to the confusing assembly of four of his brothers, Sawyer, Cort, Rafe and Josh and Cort's wife Laurel and their four children, Tommy, Angela, Sophia and Quin, was beginning to feel overwhelming. The oldest brother, Cruz, had called to say he'd be a little late for the family meeting, and Duran could only be thankful for one less person in the room and hope he'd be coming alone.

Noah lingered at his side, looking both intimidated and excited. He stared wide-eyed as Tommy, who seemed to Duran to be about twelve or thirteen, played the role of Bigfoot, chasing his much younger siblings around the room. His son was used to a quiet house and often only his imagination and toys for company. He could feel Noah fairly quivering with anticipation, wanting to join in and yet unsure of whether he could or should.

Sidestepping out of the way as one of the girls dodged around him, Rafe gave Duran a knowing look. "Be glad we left the other ankle biters at home," he commented with a shake of his head. "When they're all together, it's a lot worse."

Duran briefly wondered exactly how many of them there were and then thought of Ry. From the little time he'd spent with his twin, he got the impression that for Ry, family ties—ties to anyone—were something to be avoided at all costs. He suspected for Ry, a meeting like this would be akin to slow torture.

"Tommy, why don't you take Noah out and show him the new foal?" Laurel made the suggestion over the rising ruckus in the ranch great room, giving an exasperated shake of her head when it went unacknowledged by her oldest son. She turned to Duran. "Would that be all right with you? There's a brand new baby on the ranch and she's just beautiful."

"I don't—I'm not sure Noah is up to a long walk right now," he hedged, trying for a diplomatic way to say no. Though he didn't doubt Laurel meant well, he wasn't ready to entrust his son to people he'd barely met, related or not.

Silently urging her to back him up he glanced at Lia, sitting to the other side of Noah.

He'd argued with himself, even up to the moment he was standing at the front door of the ranch, over whether her coming along was a good idea or not. He'd wanted her there, for Noah's sake and his own.

She was Noah's pediatrician, at least while they were here. Noah had had other doctors, but he sensed Lia cared more deeply for Noah. And that counted for a lot. Besides, he wanted her there, for Noah's sake and his own, because her empathy for their situation and her knowing his brothers and Jed Garrett eased the difficulties of first meetings and explanations. Although they'd disagreed over his staying at the ranch, in his mind she was still his strongest supporter here, and he hoped in this, her understanding of the situation would lead her to add her own objections to Laurel's suggestion.

"Can I go, Dad?" Noah tugged at his sleeve. "I feel fine now. Dr. Kerrigan said I was fine." He turned to Lia in hopeful appeal.

"I said you were better," Lia amended gently. Over Noah's head, her eyes met Duran's. "I don't think a short walk would hurt, as long as you took it slow. But it's up to your dad. He might want you to keep him company since he's in a strange place and doesn't really know anybody."

"You're here. He knows you," Noah persisted. "Please, Dad. I want to go."

"Noah—" His first instinct to say no battled with wanting to let Noah explore and enjoy being a part of a group of kids. It so rarely happened and he hated that his son had spent so much of his short life lonely.

"Please?" Noah looked over to where Tommy in his role of Bigfoot with Quin, a sturdy toddler, clinging to his back, was about to pounce on his little sisters and then at Duran with that wide-eyed pleading expression that never failed to break the back of Duran's resolve.

"You don't have to worry about Tommy," Josh put in. "He's as good as Rafe and me at knowin' his way around the ranch.

And since he's the oldest, he's had lots of practice at keepin' an eye on the littler ones."

"Tommy's very responsible," Laurel added, a touch of pride in her voice. Tommy's mock ferocious snarl elicited high-pitched shrieks from the girls and Laurel winced. "Okay, enough. Tommy—stop growling." She walked over and scooped up Quin. "The girls are getting completely out of control. Why don't you take them and Noah on a walk to the barn and show Noah the new filly? Slowly, though, Noah just got out of the hospital."

"Sure." Tommy gestured to Noah, "Come on, let's get outta here."

"Take your sisters by the hand," Cort insisted. "Don't let them wander off."

"Come on, Dad, they can—"

"Tommy."

Cort's tone was enough to silence his son. "Fine, I'll take Angela and you take Sophie," he told Noah, gently pushing the smallest girl toward him.

For a moment, Sophie contemplated Noah with big black eyes and then grinned. Noah looked to Duran and Duran smiled. "It's okay. Take her hand and stay close. And no running, okay?"

Hesitantly, Noah pushed off the couch and stood there, staring at Sophie as if he wasn't sure what part of her to hold on to.

With none of Noah's reticence, Sophie grabbed his hand and tugged. "Let's go see the pony!"

Then Noah beamed back and Duran knew he'd made the right choice. "No longer than an hour," he said as his son let Sophie pull him toward the front door.

"You keep track of the time, Tommy," Cort called to his son as the four kids made a noisy exit.

"He'll be fine." Without him noticing, Lia had shifted a little closer and spoke only for him, following his gaze to the empty place his son had just left.

She touched his hand, a brief brush of her fingers, intended to punctuate her reassurance, and for a moment, Duran had the urge to grasp hers as if she were the tether that would keep him anchored above the confusion of feelings and people and remind him of what was important.

Instead, he let the feeling pass and settled for a half nod, half shrug.

Although she smiled a little in return, her eyes were troubled. She answered some comment of Laurel's but Duran felt and saw her watching him, slantways, pretending her attention was elsewhere but keeping him in view in a way that was almost protective.

Before he could decide how he felt about that, the front door flung open and a man strode in to join the company. From his strong resemblance to Sawyer and Cort, Duran guessed this was Cruz Déclan, his opinion justified a moment later when the man walked up and offered his hand as Duran got to his feet.

"You must be Duran," he said. "I'm Cruz. Welcome to the family."

The words were friendly enough but came with a wry twist that gave Duran the impression Cruz understood some of how he felt about being the outsider who suddenly found himself a part of a tight-knit family group.

Taking a chair opposite Duran, Cruz asked, "Looks like I beat Jed here." He looked to Cort. "I heard you got voted the one to make the call last night. How'd he take it?"

"Like we expected," Cort said. "Del on the other hand—"

"She isn't takin' it too well," Josh finished for him.

Sawyer gave a short laugh. "Now there's an understatement. Del is Josh's mother," he added for Duran's benefit. "So we're gonna let him handle her."

"Just don't take it personally if she's less than warm and fuzzy," Josh said, with an apologetic smile Duran's way.

"I understand. It's a difficult situation. If there'd been any other way—"

"We're glad you found us," Laurel said. She gently stroked Quin's back where he lay, snuggled against her chest. "If there's any chance one of us could help Noah…" Leaving the sentence unfinished, she looked at Quin, shaking her head, her eyes misty.

"I think we can all understand how you feel when it comes to your son," Sawyer said quietly.

"I'll get things lined up for the testing next week," Lia said. "I know everyone here is more than willing."

Duran's brothers all nodded and made comments in full agreement. Their enthusiasm and open acceptance of him and Noah, and Lia's determination to help him find what he most wanted for his son, wrapped around an empty place inside, warming it and filling it with feelings too tangled to recognize. For a moment, he couldn't speak, gripped by a sense that he'd found a lot more than he'd ever bargained for here.

Before he could muster words of thanks around the catch in his throat, the front door opened again. And again, Duran recognized the features on the man's face. Not so much because he strongly resembled any of his sons in the room, but because he was looking at an image of Ry—older, grayer, harder, but a reflection of his twin.

The clear proof of his identity was there and now he had to confront it face-to-face in the man who was his father.

Chapter Four

They stood facing each other and there didn't seem to be a right thing to say.

The sense of imbalance Duran had been feeling since he started the search for his birth parents visited him now, more strongly than ever. He'd always been confident of who he was, where he belonged. The confrontations with his past, though, had stirred to life a stranger inside; someone, that if it hadn't been for Noah, he wasn't certain he would have wanted to know.

"Not sure what I expected," Jed said at last. He came slowly into the room until he faced Duran. His blunt assessing look ended with a grunt and a shake of his head. "But it wasn't you."

"That's pretty much what Ry said," Duran told him, despite the circumstances a little amused at the similar reaction from his twin and the father neither of them had ever known. "You'd have a hard time guessing we were twins. There's no question he's your son, though. You're more his twin than I am, at least in looks."

Jed accepted that with a nod. "Who's your mama?"

"Lucy Miller, or she was then. And the only place she's my mother is on a birth certificate."

"Maybe so. But you can't change where you came from. Believe me, boy, I've tried." Eyes narrowed as if he were peering into the past, Jed said after a moment, "I don't recall a Lucy Miller."

"One-night stands generally don't leave much of an impression," Duran said dryly. "She probably wouldn't have remembered you, either, if you hadn't given her two sons."

"When?" The question was shot at Duran from behind Jed and for the first time Duran noticed the blond woman, fluffy white poodle clutched in her arm, still standing by the doorway. Duran guessed she had to be Jed's wife, Del. When Duran didn't answer her straightaway, Del spun on Jed. "When did you know her?"

"Like I said, I can't recall. What's it matter?"

Del's painted mouth tightened. "People will be talking."

"Let 'em. Not like they haven't before."

From the hard set of her face, Duran guessed whatever had been said about Jed Garrett in the past hadn't been good. He had a pretty fair idea of what they'd be talking about this time, the speculation over whether or not Jed and Del had been married when Jed's night with a stranger had produced two more Garrett sons. Judging Josh's age as fairly close to his, there was a better than even chance they had. He couldn't blame Del Garrett for resenting his suddenly showing up in Luna Hermosa. For Jed's wife, meeting him face-to-face was unwelcome evidence her husband had cheated on her.

Before Del could counter Jed, though, Josh came up and

took his mother by the arm. "How 'bout you come over to my place and tell Ellie and me all about your trip?" Del's protesting didn't start until Josh had her turned around and halfway out the door. Flashing a wink and a grin over his shoulder, he pulled the door closed on his mother's increasingly loud sputtering.

"Damned woman's gonna make a fuss about this," Jed grumbled as he made his way to a chair, dropping heavily into the seat. He sent a scowl around the room at each of his sons, sparing only Duran. "And don't any of you start. I'll get enough grief from her to make up for the lot of you." He fixed his attention back on Duran. "Cort says you're here about your boy. What makes you so sure one of your brothers can help?"

"Because they are his brothers," Lia spoke for him.

Duran had forgotten she was there behind him, now at his side, squarely facing Jed in a stance that clearly warned the older man to back off. He didn't need her to fight his battles but she ignored his glance.

"A blood relative is more likely to be a match," she persisted. "And if one of them is, it can save Noah's life."

"And then what?"

Lia bristled but Duran took her hand, squeezing lightly, trying to telegraph his appreciation for her defense in equal measure with insistence he handle this on his own.

"You either get what you want or you don't," Jed went on. "Is that gonna be the end of it?"

"You're asking for something I can't give right now," Duran said, not knowing if Jed wanted him to say he'd stick around, acknowledge these strangers as family, but suspecting Jed wanted a commitment of that sort. Whether or not Jed had that in mind, Duran couldn't promise, not now, maybe never.

"Let it go for now," Cruz told Jed, undeterred by his father's obvious irritation at his interruption. "Duran has enough to worry about without taking on all of us on top of it."

Jed looked as if he wanted to argue. But after a moment, he shifted his glare from Cruz back to Duran. His gaze was speculative, and Duran realized he still held Lia's hand and that she hadn't made any attempt to let him go. Gently, Duran loosed his grip, briefly meeting her eyes before he broke their connection.

"I want to meet your brother," Jed said. "Why isn't he here?"

"This has got nothing to do with Ry. I don't know him that well, but he doesn't strike me as the social type. He wasn't exactly thrilled to find out about me, let alone a whole family. We agreed we'd keep in touch but we haven't gotten much further than that."

"Your mama should've told me about you two."

"Would it have made a difference?" Duran asked shortly. "Then?"

"Might've. I guess it makes more now." Jed rubbed a hand over his jaw and weariness seemed to wash over him, weighing down his shoulders and taking the aggression out of his stance. He pushed himself to his feet. "Get settled in. We'll talk more at dinner."

Duran almost said no, thanks, he wasn't staying, this wasn't what he'd bargained on when he'd come to Luna Hermosa looking for help. But before he could voice any of it, Noah and his cousins came back in a burst of noise and energy. His focus turned to his son's excited telling of his visit to the barns, and seeing the horses and a family of cats.

Seeing Noah's excitement reminded him of why he was here and that it didn't matter what price he had to pay for coming. The only thing that mattered to Duran was that Noah had a chance at a normal, happy life, free of hospitals and worries about what tomorrow would bring…that his son had a chance to live.

Lia decided that at some point in her life, she must have been forced to endure a worse dinner party, but she couldn't remember when.

Once Noah returned and the family gathering started to break up, she'd planned to leave and avoid any more time with Jed and Del Garrett. A scant half an hour after Josh had led her away, Del had come back to the house, more upset than before, and flounced off to find Jed when she learned Duran and Noah would be temporary houseguests. Lia could only imagine the scene that followed and was more than ready to excuse herself for home.

It was Duran who stopped her.

She'd been surprised when he asked her to stay. But she accepted, deliberately refusing to think too much about her motivation, certain little about it was professional.

She let herself wonder about his reasons, though. She supposed it could have been as simple as wanting the support of the person he knew best in Luna Hermosa, though he and she were hardly much more than strangers. Apart from that, he'd given her the message several times that he didn't need her involved in his personal life beyond her caring for Noah.

All through dinner he left her wondering, contributing little to the conversations, volunteering even less, particularly in response to Jed's questioning. Cort, ever the family peace-maker, had done his best to smooth over the tensions, and the five kids provided some diversions. But Duran seemed distracted, his attention inward. Del was obviously in a temper and as a consequence, Jed was surlier than ever. Shortly after dinner, Cort and Laurel departed for home and Duran, seeing Noah's yawns and eye rubbing, whisked him off to bed.

That left Lia in the awkward position of not wanting to leave without saying something to Duran, but not wanting to stay if it meant lingering in Del and Jed's company. She finally settled on thanking them and then saying she wanted to check on Noah before she, too, went home.

Quickly navigating the long hallway that led to the west wing of the house, Lia tapped lightly on the door at the end of it, waiting for a few moments before Duran answered.

"I'm sorry," he said, as he showed her in. "I didn't mean to abandon you."

"It's okay. I just wanted to make sure Noah was all right before I left. And to say good-night."

"He's finally sleeping." Duran glanced back at the closed door of one of the bedrooms. "It took awhile. He was tired but he's had too much excitement for one day."

"He seemed to enjoy himself, though. I think it was good for him to be with the other kids."

"Is that your professional opinion?" Duran asked with a slight smile.

"It could be." There were long moments of silence, weighted with things unsaid, and then Lia took a step back. "I should go. I'll call you later about the testing once I've gotten a firm commitment on the time."

"Lia…" In the dim light, his expression was unreadable, but she sensed his hesitation. "I know I keep asking, but would you stay? For just a little while? There's a patio outside…" He let the suggestion trail off, leaving it to her to decide if any of this was a good idea.

She told herself there were no decisions to make—it was a bad idea, them alone together in a situation that could easily be misconstrued. Yet she succumbed too easily to the temptation to say yes and was nodding and following him out to the patio before the voice telling her to turn and leave could sound the alarm.

At the height of summer, the day's heat had been brilliant, but in the deep evening darkness, the warmth had softened, tempered by a light breeze. Duran moved to stand by the low wall surrounding the patio, staring at the blended expanse of land and sky spread in front of them.

Uncertain of his mood, Lia tentatively approached him, taking a seat on the low wall a little distance from him. He hadn't bothered with lights so she saw him largely in shadow, faintly lit by the dim aura of the lamp in the room behind and the pale glow of full moonlight in front.

"I hope this wasn't a mistake," he said, more to himself than to her.

"I don't think so," she said quietly. "This can be a good place, for you and for Noah. It could be healing in itself."

"I'd say after today, the verdict is out on whether or not this is a good place for either of us," he said, not looking at her.

"I didn't mean here—the ranch—so much." She followed his gaze. "I meant Luna Hermosa. It's why I've stayed for so long. It's the only place that's ever felt like home."

"You didn't grow up here?"

"I didn't grow up in any one place. My parents split up when I was three and I got bounced between the two of them. My mother in particular doesn't like staying in one spot for too long." The bitter edge to her words surprised her although she knew she'd been hoarding it up for years now. Quickly, she tried to bury it again, unwilling to expose her skeletons to Duran Forrester. "It doesn't matter now. I hadn't been here very long before I decided to adopt it as home."

"I doubt Noah and I will ever call it home, but I'm going to give it a few days. At least until we know the test results."

"I'll try and make that happen as quickly as possible. I can imagine how you feel about having to wait, but if we can get everyone tested on Tuesday, we should know something by the end of next week, at the latest."

He turned to her then. "I appreciate everything you've done, that you're doing."

"But…?"

"I wasn't going to qualify it."

"Not out loud. But I have the impression you think I've stepped in where I shouldn't have. That I've gotten too involved in your personal business. Maybe I have," she said before he could answer her. She could hear herself, knew she was doing what Nova had accused her of—throwing up obstacles to protect herself from getting in any deeper with Duran and his son. Standing up, she instinctively shifted toward the light and escape.

"Maybe you have," Duran said, his flat agreement startling her, holding her in place. Then, with mingled regret and relief, when she thought she might be able to leave without having to confront her feelings, he knocked aside all her barriers with ridiculous ease. "But you care and I think you understand—"

"What it's like to be afraid of losing someone you love?" she finished for him, and at his nod, thought, *Oh, if you only knew.*

"Duran…" She didn't know what she was asking him, whether to stop or to continue.

He moved closer, close enough she had to look up to meet his steady gaze. Close enough for him to reach out, slowly, and trace his fingertips over her cheek.

"You're not the only one who's gone where they shouldn't have," he said softly.

"I don't—" *What? Feel this much, want this much, because of a man I hardly know?* Unsettled, agitated by what she didn't understand and her inability to control it, she finished, "I don't know how to handle what's happened between us. I didn't expect to—care the way I do."

"Neither did I. But it doesn't seem to matter."

"It's the situation—Noah, and the timing, and your family," she rushed out, grasping for a sensible explanation. "It makes everything seem more intense than it is."

Looking doubtful, he said, "That's part of it."

"And you're grateful—"

"I'm not that damned grateful, Lia."

"You needed someone and I wanted to help."

"No. That's not it."

Before she could find another reason to convince him that whatever imagined connection between them was nothing more than the heightened emotion of the circumstances, Duran slid his hand around her nape and kissed her.

She wanted it and it scared the hell out of her at the same time because of how much she wanted it. She could tell herself all day it was comfort he needed and she provided, but the feeling—too basic, too elemental—made that a lie. It was desire, although definitely not pure or simple. For long moments, she indulged it, leaning into his warmth, opening her mouth to his, taking as much as she gave because she knew it couldn't last.

Stopping it herself would have been best. Instead, Duran abruptly ended it, letting her go and taking a step back. He looked slightly stunned, as if he couldn't believe what he'd just done. "Lia—"

"Forget it." Unable to look him straight in the eye, she turned away. Running a hand over her hair, she was annoyed to find it trembling. "It doesn't mean anything."

"Do you really believe that?" The demand for honesty in his voice compelled her to face him.

"No," she answered truthfully, "but I need to try. I shouldn't—none of this is very professional of me."

"It hasn't been very *professional* between us from the beginning."

"And that makes it okay?"

"No, it complicates the hell out of things," he said bluntly. "But it doesn't change the way they are."

He was right but she didn't want him to be; she wanted to pretend she could ignore it, dismiss it and move on. Duran and her own feelings wouldn't let her.

Brushing her hand with his, he drew her eyes back to his. "We don't have to figure it all out tonight. Just don't expect me to pretend it didn't happen."

Lia shook her head, the only answer she could give him, and she wasn't sure if she was agreeing or denying him. Both felt like the wrong choice.

Chapter Five

"I'm sorry to keep you waiting so long." Lia hurried into the pediatrician's patient room, interrupting Duran's agitated pacing. "Overscheduling seems to be the rule these days," she said, closing the door behind her.

The tension radiating from him was like a living thing in the room. He offered her little more than a terse nod in reply.

"Noah's not with you?"

"Josh and Eliana offered to look after him while we talked. They're meeting me here later," he said tightly. "You said you'd rather talk to me alone."

He didn't look happy with that, but Lia knew it was better this way. "Did they bring Sammy along?" she asked, thinking Eliana's little brother, only a year older than Noah, would have helped distract Noah from being away from his father again.

"Yeah, Noah was excited. He can't get enough of his new family. Look, Lia, can we avoid the chitchat and get on with it? It's been over a week and I don't do waiting well, especially when it comes to this."

Lia drew in a breath. She had rehearsed since the moment she'd gotten the results of his brothers' blood tests. She had to make it clear that while there was hope, she could promise nothing at this point. And, despite the feelings, real or imagined, that had passed between Duran and her, first and foremost, she had to remain professional.

But more and more that obligation was becoming a challenge that was harder to meet. She'd deliberately avoided close contact with Duran in the past days, making sure the few times she did see him were because of Noah and always at the hospital or her office. It didn't make it any easier to ignore the attraction between them and to pretend he'd never kissed her. She couldn't ignore or forget, not with him ever present in her thoughts, despite her best efforts to relegate him to a safe father-of-patient status only.

He was watching her now with barely concealed impatience. Putting herself in doctor mode, she said, "I have good news."

Duran stared at her, frozen in place, as if he were waiting for a blow and certain she was going to take her words back. "Go on."

"Sawyer is a match for Noah."

He said nothing, just stood there.

"It's true, Duran," Lia said softly. Moving close to him, she put a gentle hand on his arm. "Sawyer's tests came back as a perfect match. There's a very good chance he'll be able to be a donor for Noah."

A tremor passed over him and he swayed slightly, causing Lia to grab for the nearest chair and pull it near enough for him to collapse into it.

"I—I can't believe…" he rasped. "All this time—and finally…" He leaned forward and dropped his head to his hands.

An ache tightened her chest and throat, threatening to become tears. All these years of fear and anguished waiting, wondering if and when he would lose his son forever. Had he ever truly let himself believe Noah had a chance for a normal life? Or had he resigned himself to the inevitable, certain that with so few close blood family members, the chance Noah would find a compatible donor in time was virtually impossible?

It wasn't professional or even wise, but she didn't care as she knelt beside him and put her arm around him; her instinct to comfort him was stronger than any common sense dictated.

His body shook with his effort to bank the tumult of emotions she knew he must be feeling. It touched her in a way for which she had no response except to tighten her hold, to offer him an anchor in the storm.

"It's okay," she murmured, stroking his hair. "You don't always have to be strong. And you don't always have to do it alone."

"I told myself I had hope," he said hoarsely. "That I believed this would happen." He raised his head to look at her then, and his eyes were glazed with unshed tears. "When I couldn't find a donor, though, and they told me it could be years, or never…" Leaning back in his chair, he squeezed his eyes shut, shoving his hands through his hair. "I wasn't strong enough to believe it then."

"Oh, Duran." Lia touched her fingers to his face to bring his gaze to hers. "Noah has an excellent chance now. Once Sawyer knows, I'm certain he'll more than willing to do whatever is necessary to help."

His expression wavered, caught between desperately wanting to believe and being afraid it was all a mistake. "You're sure?"

"Yes, I'm sure," she said firmly, her smile tempered by the

need to be realistic with him. "But you realize this is only the first step along a long, rocky road ahead. They'll be more tests and the transplant procedure itself, then the recovery time for Noah—none of it's going to be short or easy."

"But it is *the* first step, isn't it? At last… Lia—" He caught her hands in his. "Thank you."

Now it was her turn to try to contain a whirl of emotion— empathy for his years of waiting, relief that the test results opened up new possibilities, a fierce happiness knowing Duran's faith had been renewed—so many feelings rushing her heart that if she tried to speak them it would be through tears. So she only nodded, and said quietly, "All I've done is arrange the testing. You're the reason you and Noah have gotten this far."

"You've done a lot more than that." He shook his head, a dazed look in his eyes. "It's still hard to believe that I came here looking for my father and found five brothers and now one of them is going to save Noah's life."

Lia ached to echo his newfound certainty, but didn't dare. Duran needed to be positive now. His mindset would determine Noah's attitude and that in turn would give Noah strength. But she had to keep a balance, stating the truth in careful terms, cautioning Duran, yet encouraging him in equal measure. From now on it would be a delicate line to walk, especially given the other complications of her burgeoning attraction to him and her deepening affection for his little boy.

"It's true. Sawyer is a match and he may very well be the one to help Noah get well. But we've got dozens of details to work out now. You need to start by finding a transplant clinic. You may have to go out of state for that. But there is one in Albuquerque. There's another in Dallas. I'll be glad to liaison for you, but that decision is yours. And keep in mind, the wait time for the actual transplant could be several weeks and

Noah's recovery will be a lot longer." She backed away and drew herself to her feet. "What I'm saying is that this is good news, but you both have a long way to go yet."

"I know. I've read everything I could get my hands on for years." Duran stood up, walked across the room over to the sink and splashed his face with cold water. He grabbed a paper towel from the holder and turned back to her. "I'll do whatever it takes, however long it takes."

Lia nodded, not trusting herself to speak as she tried to banish thoughts of the myriad of things that could go wrong. Duran needed to know them all, but not today. Right now, it was more important he believe in everything that could go right. "Are you ready to talk to Noah?"

"Oh, yeah," he said, and for the first time he smiled.

In the waiting room, they found Noah and Sammy sitting happily at a children's table playing video games and making all manner of boy sound effects. Josh and Eliana sat nearby watching them. They looked up simultaneously as Lia and Duran walked into the room.

"Dad!" Noah bounced up and ran over to them when he spotted Duran. "Sammy has that new game I was telling you about. It's way awesome, come check it out."

Duran swept his son into his arms and hugged him as though he would never let him go. "Sure, in a minute, okay?" he said, his voice breaking a little.

"What's wrong?" Noah squirmed in his father's embrace. "You're squashing me."

"Sorry, I guess I was." Duran released his son, keeping his hands on his shoulders. "I missed you, that's all. Did you have fun?"

"Yeah, we went to the video store. I found three games I want," he added with a hopeful look.

"No doubt," Duran said with a chuckle. "We'll see about that later."

Noah's mouth twisted. "That always means no," he grumbled. Wriggling out of Duran's hold, he ran back to the table to watch over Sammy's shoulder as the older boy manipulated the game with quick fingers.

"So, you gonna keep us in suspense?" Josh asked when Noah was out of earshot.

Lia and Duran exchanged a glance and he nodded slightly, giving her tacit permission. "Sawyer's a match," she said, giving them a brief outline of what she'd told Duran.

Eliana, her eyes bright, caught Duran by surprise with a warm hug. "That's wonderful. We've all been hoping and praying this would happen. I can only imagine how awful the waiting's been for you."

"Noah's got a long way to go yet." Lia repeated her gentle warning. She smiled at Duran. "But this is a very good start."

"Does Sawyer know yet?" Eliana asked.

"No, I'm going to call him as soon as we're done here. I'm sure he'll be happy."

"'Course he will, you know that," Josh said, including Duran in his assurance. "We all are."

Duran glanced at his son and then turned his smile to his brother and Eliana. "I appreciate everything you've all done. I'll admit I had doubts about coming here but right now, it's looking like the best decision I've ever made."

"Good thing, since you're stuck with us all now," Josh said with a laugh. "Hey, you think Noah would be up for a little celebration? I promised Sammy we'd go ridin' today. Cort and Tommy'll be there, and Anna. Ellie's little sister," he added for Duran's benefit. "She and Tommy are sweet on each other."

Eliana grimaced. "They're just kids."

"They're teenagers and if Tommy's anything like I was…" He finished with a grin and a shrug as Eliana muttered, "God forbid," and rolled her eyes. "So, what do you say?" Josh asked. "You and Noah wanna come along? You, too, Lia. We'll make it a real party."

"I don't know," both Lia and Duran started at the same time. He gestured her to go ahead and she said, "I'm going to be tied up here until at least three. I'm sure Noah would enjoy the outing, though, if you think he's up to it."

Duran hesitated then said, "I need to talk to Noah first, explain to him what's going on." He looked at Lia. "Would you—"

"Of course," she answered his unspoken request. Josh and Eliana agreed to wait while she and Duran took Noah back to the patient room to tell Noah about the test results and to decide on the afternoon's plans.

It was easier, this time, telling Noah the news, because all she had to do was echo Duran's explanation, adding a few words of encouragement. She was pretty sure Noah didn't hear anything beyond Duran telling him Sawyer was a match anyway.

What she hadn't been prepared for, though, was the rush of emotion when Noah flung himself at her for an enthusiastic hug.

"I'm gonna get better!"

Lia returned his hug, swallowed her tears and put on a smile for him. "We're going to do everything we can to make that happen."

"You're the best doctor ever," Noah told her, grinning from ear to ear.

"I don't know about that. Your uncle Sawyer is going to be doing more than me. But thank you." She blinked hard as she gently brushed a wayward lock of hair from his forehead. "I think you're pretty special, too."

She was glad for the reprieve when Duran repeated Josh's invitation to go riding. Noah was practically glowing with excitement.

"Can we go now?" he asked. "'Cept—" He frowned. "I don't know how to ride a horse. I only ride bikes."

Lia laughed and gently ruffled his hair. "You don't need to know how. You can ride with your dad or maybe Josh will find you a gentle older horse who's not in any hurry. Do you like to ride?" she asked Duran.

He shrugged. "I've enjoyed it the few times I've done it but I can't say I'm any cowboy. I'm a cyclist and so is Noah."

"That won't be a problem. Josh gives riding lessons to special-needs kids like Sammy. He's good at matching people and horses."

"Can everybody come?" Noah asked. "All my cousins?"

"Not today," Duran said with a smile. "And we're not going anywhere ourselves until after you've had lunch and a nap. I want to call your grandparents, too, and give them the news."

Noah's grumbled objections accompanied them back into the waiting room, abating only when Josh told him it would be late afternoon before everyone else could go, too.

"I've got to put in a couple of hours at the school," Josh said, referring to the training center for would-be rodeo riders he and a friend had launched several months ago. "And Cort and Tommy are givin' Rafe a hand around the ranch. Why don't we meet at four? We can ride down to the pond and let the kids mess around awhile and then you can come back to our place for dinner. That work for you, Lia?"

"You're coming, right?" Noah looked at her and then glanced to his dad.

Lia saw the hesitation cross Duran's face. It was all still so new, his brothers, nephews and nieces, her—probably her more than anything else. She sensed his uneasiness and the last thing she wanted was to add to it. "I'd love to, but—"

"Great, then it's settled," Josh broke in.

Doubting it, at least in Duran's case, Lia nearly made the excuse of work to back out of it. The excitement and expectation in Noah's eyes gave her pause. She hated to disappoint the little boy and at the same time she didn't want to make things harder for his father.

"It sounds good," Duran answered before she could say anything. He looked at her, his slight smile rueful. "Are you okay with that?"

She knew he was asking about more than the afternoon's plans and she really wanted to ask him the question in return. But there didn't seem to be a good way to do that in front of Josh and Eliana. "I guess I could take a few hours off this afternoon. My last appointment is at three and I'm not on call today."

"Then it's a date," Duran told Josh. "And thanks for everything."

"Hey, you know we're here for you and Noah, don't you? I know it's not been easy, gettin' used to havin' so much family all at once. But I meant what I said before, you're stuck with us all now."

Eliana smiled warmly, "And that does mean all of us."

They said their goodbyes then, gathering up Sammy and leaving Duran and Lia to face each other.

"I hope you know that I'm here for you and Noah, too, however I can help," she said.

"Is that professionally or personally?"

"I—"

"Never mind." He shook his head as if irritated at himself for asking her. He looked at her a long moment, the intensity of his searching gaze making Lia want to look away before he saw too much. Then he said softly, "I know I've said it before, but thank you." Leaning to her, he brushed a kiss over her cheek.

Warmth spread through her from his light touch and for a second she let herself savor the feel of his mouth against hers and for so much more.

"Are you done? Can we go now?" Noah interrupted. "I wanna go ride the horses."

Noah's protest broke their spell and they laughed and moved apart.

"Come on, pal," Duran said, taking Noah by the hand, "let's get out of here so Dr. Kerrigan can get back to work."

Lia bent and gave Noah a hug. "We'll be talking again about some exciting things for you soon. For today, though, I'll just finish up here so I can meet you at the ranch later."

"We'll be looking forward to it," Duran said and after all her doubts about whether or not he wanted her there, Lia believed it was true.

Chapter Six

"All saddled up and ready to ride," Josh said with a brisk slap to the plump old paint's rump. "Peggy here will do just fine for you, Noah. She's used to goin' nice and slow. Anna never had a bit of trouble with her when she was learnin' to ride."

"This is my horse," Sammy, sitting atop a smaller mare, proudly pointed out to Noah. "Her name is Sarah. I always ride her."

Nearby, Cort was helping Tommy lengthen his stirrup, Anna watching from the horse beside them. "If you keep growing like this, we're gonna have to find you a new saddle." He turned to Duran. "Just wait until Noah hits his teens. You can't keep 'em clothed or fed."

Duran had rarely let himself indulge in imaging Noah as a teenager. The thought that he might never see his son grow up always quelled his visions. But now, could he dare to indulge in thinking of, even planning for Noah's future? Every cell in his body screamed yes, but the euphoria of hearing Sawyer was a match was dispelling, leaving in its wake all-too-familiar fears. At the hospital all he could feel was hope. After even a few short hours of mulling things over, letting the news sink in, reason declared war on blind optimism.

He distanced himself from the raging conflict of emotions, not willing to air them to his brothers, and simply answered Cort with a noncommittal, "So I've heard."

Cort stopped what he was doing and laid a hand on Duran's shoulder. Duran tensed, but it didn't seem to discourage Cort. "You'll find out. Josh told me the great news about Sawyer."

"It is good news," Duran said, thinking how inadequate his words were compared to his feelings. "I'm still a little over-whelmed, I guess."

"I can see why. But you've got the best pediatrician in town on your team." Both men turned to catch Lia a few feet away throwing one long, slender leg over her mount. "And she's not a half-bad horsewoman either."

Lia, not knowing they were talking about her, threaded the reins through her fingers. "Where are your girls and your little boy today?" she called over to Cort.

"Quin had a playdate and the girls are at ballet. Angela would have gladly skipped it to come riding, but Laurel wouldn't hear of it. That's what they get for having a teacher for a mother. Laurel would consider it an insult to another teacher to let her daughter ditch class."

"Too bad for them," Tommy said, slanting a grin at Anna. "They're gonna be jealous we got to go."

Cort gave Tommy a stern look. "No rubbing it in or next time you'll be sitting in on ballet class."

The threat made Noah giggle. "That would be way funny."

"Ha, ha," Tommy shot back.

Finishing Tommy's stirrups, Cort turned back to Duran. "I know you keep hearing this, but anything Laurel and I can do—" he paused "—anything at all. We're here."

"I told him he was stuck with us," Josh added as he lifted Noah onto Peggy's back. He gave Noah a quick lesson on how to steady himself and stay upright, then swung into the saddle of his own mount.

Duran appreciated the gesture; he still couldn't believe how readily and easily his brothers had accepted him, Noah and their situation. It almost seemed too good to be true, and a big part of him feared it was. While none of his brothers had said or done anything to justify his doubts yet, he had long abandoned the habit of relying on anyone else for support or comfort.

And that's why you keep spilling everything to Lia? Because you don't share, you don't rely on anyone?

He caught her watching him and the slight questioning expression on her face made him wonder what she'd read in his. Shaking off his introspection, he looked between Cort and Josh and said, "I don't know how to thank you, all of you."

"By helpin' us get these kids to the pond." Josh pointed to a wooded area to the east. "We'll keep it to a walk, since it's your first time, Noah."

"Can we go already?" Noah insisted, wriggling excitedly in his saddle.

Duran watched his eager son, reins in hand, looking as comfortable and confident on Peggy as a boy who'd grown up on a ranch. "Stay close to Dr. Kerrigan and me, okay?"

"Tommy, you and Anna keep an eye on Noah, same as you do with Angela," Cort called after his son, who'd already taken the group's lead.

Tommy waved him off over his shoulder and let out an exaggerated sigh. "I know, I know."

"Don't worry," Josh said, "Noah will be fine. Peggy's real good with kids and she knows her way to the pond. All Noah's gotta do is hold on."

Wanting to believe Josh, Duran nodded, but the protective father in him wouldn't rest easy again until Peggy was back in the barn and Noah was safely on solid ground.

Once started in the right direction, the group of them fell into a comfortable pattern, the kids riding a little ahead, he and Lia side by side behind them, Cort and Josh bringing up the rear. Duran began to relax a bit, soak in the sun and breathtaking high country scenery. It was then he was finally able to focus his attention on Lia.

She fairly glowed beneath the afternoon sun, her hair threaded with a thousand different highlights of copper and gold, her cheeks flushed soft pink, a slight smile curving her lips as she savored the air fragrant with pinion and sage.

"You ride well," he said, taking note of the curve of her backside and thighs beneath slim jeans as her body rose and fell in harmony with her horse's rhythm.

"Me? No, hardly," she said with a chuckle. "I've never had time to pursue it as a sport or a hobby. Medical school, then my practice pretty much precluded getting good at any sports."

"You could have fooled me. You ride like a natural."

"You're not doing so badly yourself for someone not used to a horse."

They smiled at each other. "I haven't fallen off yet, so I guess that's progress. I have to admit, this is a nice change. My preferred mode of transport is my bicycle. In California, I hardly use a car. Now that Noah is old enough to ride with me, when he's feeling up to it, we bike everywhere together."

"What a great thing to do together. Did you grow up riding bikes a lot?"

Nodding, Duran remembered his childhood fondly. "Yeah, my dad got me into it. We used to spend endless hours messing around in the garage, building bikes, taking them apart, getting new components and rebuilding them. He ran sort of a neighborhood bike shop out of our garage." He glanced over to Lia, noticing she had a distant look in her eyes. "I'm sorry, I'm boring you."

Lia's horse sneezed and shook all over. She bent and stroked his neck. "Almost to the pond, where you can take a rest under a shady tree," she soothed. Slowly, she turned toward Duran, a strangely solemn look on her face. "You're not boring me at all," she answered softly. "I'm imagining what it must have been like growing up with parents who spent so much time with you, and thinking how lucky Noah is to have such a devoted father."

The few things she'd said, the old pain underlying her words, made him wonder, yet hesitant to ask directly about her childhood. It might be something she wasn't comfortable talking about with him. But curiosity got the best of him and he asked straight out, "I get the impression you aren't that close to your parents."

Lia laughed, but it was a brittle sound, without joy. "That would be the understatement of the century. I spent very little time with my parents. They were far too occupied messing up their lives to waste time trying to improve ours. I taught myself to ride a bike, finally, out of embarrassment at being the last kid on the block to learn, at about Noah's age. I fell so many times, my knees still have scars. Neither of my parents had time to help me. Between work, destroying their marriage, divorce, remarriage, boyfriends and girlfriends, kids were mostly an inconvenient blip in their social schedules."

Duran could barely conceive that kind of life, although he

wasn't naive enough to think it didn't exist. He'd been lucky.
Compared to his stable, constant, loving middle-class upbringing, her childhood sounded like a bad soap opera.

He couldn't help but wonder how years of living with in-
stability had affected her own sense of self, her ideas of love
and commitment. Red flags immediately went up and he
knew one thing for certain. He had to get to know Lia Kerrigan
a lot better before allowing his son to get any closer or invest-
ing more of himself in her.

They rode along in an awkward silence for several minutes,
the only sound a muffled clop of the horses' hooves through
tall grass. Ahead of them, the sound of the kids' talking and
laughing made happy music on the breeze.

When he turned to her, he found her watching him, her eyes
now veiled in caution. "I've scared you, haven't I? You didn't
grow up at all the way I did."

"No, I didn't. In fact, you'd probably call my life dull
compared to yours. My parents, who were quite a bit older
than is typical by the time they decided to adopt, loved me
and doted on me, but I never felt spoiled, exactly. We didn't
have a lot of money, but we did have a lot of love in our house,
Mom and Dad for each other and each of them for me. I guess
that's why I grew up being naive to the fact that all marriages
are not so idyllic." Unwillingly, the memory of the day Amber
walked out on Noah and him reared up from the dark corner
of his mind where he'd shoved it. He shook his head in remembered anger and pain. "Mine certainly wasn't."

"I'm sorry. I've never been married, but I have been
through more breakups and separations, mostly because of my
parents', than I can count. It hurts every time, especially if you
don't see it coming."

"I should have. I did, probably. I just didn't want to see it because it didn't fit the image in my head. It wasn't supposed to happen. Not to me. Not to Noah. When I married, I married for life, just like my parents. For better or for worse—all that idealistic stuff."

"And now?" Lia asked, brushing aside an errant strand of hair the light wind had blown across her cheek. "What do you believe?"

Duran watched the delicate play of her slender fingers over her smooth, flushed skin. Looking at her—strong, radiant with health and vivacity, yet soft with caring and tenderness toward him and Noah—he wanted to say he felt nothing but hope, that his beliefs were unshaken despite his ex-wife's abandonment.

But that would be a lie. The truth was his idealism had been shaken to its core. And despite the genuineness of Lia's compassion and kindness, he had to remind himself to remain on guard, to be wary even though it felt so natural to be vulnerable to her. Like no other woman he'd met, from the start something about her relaxed his usual defenses. He almost couldn't help but open himself to her, yet he knew he had to resist that impulse for Noah's sake and his.

Finally he shifted in his saddle and twisted to look at her. "I believe people still find that kind of love, the kind that lasts a lifetime. But I also believe those people are few and far between."

Lia's smile fell away, betraying her disappointment at his answer. "That's too bad. I was hoping that if anyone could have optimism about love and marriage it would be you. Because of your parents, I mean."

"I haven't totally lost it," he said lightly. "But I've definitely gotten out of the habit of thinking it's going to be a part of my life. I've been on my own for so long now that it's hard for me to imagine myself ever finding someone I'd be willing to share it with again."

"Yes…" She glanced away, focusing on the path ahead. "It's hard, when you're afraid of losing someone you love."

It wasn't exactly his meaning and at first he thought she was referring to Noah. But his next impression was that it was more about her vulnerability or one she thought they shared.

They once more fell into an uneasy silence, avoiding looking at each other, until thankfully, the kids turned around then, Tommy helping Noah swing his mount around, starting back toward them.

Pulling their horses up nose to nose with Lia and Duran's, Noah was all smiles. "The pond's up there. Can I go with everybody else?"

Cort and Josh caught up to them then and Cort grabbed Noah's reins. "We'll go with them. You and Lia can take your time."

"You won't have any trouble findin' us," Josh said with a nod toward the kids. "Just follow the noise."

"Watch me, Dad, I can ride," Noah said gleefully. With that he gave Peggy a nudge in the flanks and the old horse picked up the pace ever so slightly, following obediently in the path of the other horses.

Duran laughed at his son's enthusiasm as the group moved off, the awkwardness with Lia forgotten in his happiness at seeing Noah enjoy himself. "This was a great idea. He's having a blast. Thanks for riding out here with us."

"My pleasure," Lia said, her tone shifting from intimate friend to kindly, as if she'd put back on the mantle of professionalism.

Duran followed Lia on a path that led them out from under the beating sun on open grazing land, into a wooded hideaway. He dodged low-lying branches and scrub bushes until the dense green foliage opened up around a lush, blue pond, little shards of sunlight sparkling atop it, dancing the lazy summer afternoon away.

The rest of the group had already tethered their horses where they could sip cool water and nibble on thick grass. Noah now sat with Sammy on the edge of an old wood dock, pants rolled up, bare feet splashing in the inviting water. Anna and Tommy had already abandoned them and, after shedding their jeans, had jumped in the pond to swim.

"Can I go swimming, Dad?" Noah called out as Duran lowered himself to the ground. "Can I? I know how."

"If it's okay with you, I promised Sammy," Josh said.

"Don't worry," Cort added. "Josh and I grew up swimming here and I bring my kids all the time."

Lia, dismounting next to him, nodded to Duran's brothers. "You've got some pretty good lifeguards here."

"Go ahead," Duran told Noah. "Just stay close. I'll be right here."

With a whoop, Noah followed Sammy's example and stripped down to his boxers. Both boys jumped off the end of the dock in a cannonball that left Lia and Duran partly drenched in cold pond water.

The two boys' heads sprang up in moments. What they saw sent them bursting into uncontrolled laughter. With a quick high five, they paddled off toward a big tree with a rope swing that flew over the pond.

Lia and Duran exchanged looks, then burst out laughing, too. "They got us," Duran said. "Sorry."

"No apologies necessary," Lia said as she swiped a strand of soaked hair from her eyes. "It actually felt great. I was sweltering."

A glance passed between Cort and Josh and by some

silent agreement they moved off a few feet, eventually giving in to the calls and challenges from the kids and joining them in the water.

Still smiling, Lia turned and moved to a shady patch near a stand of trees.

Duran followed behind, unable not to notice the way her damp T-shirt clung to every curve, the way the skin was exposed as her shirt lifted when she reached up to refasten her ponytail.

She smoothed her hands over her face and neck, wiping away the last droplets of water and he wanted his hands there. The urge to touch her was so strong he had to stop himself an arm's length from her to keep from acting on his desires.

Looking up, she caught him staring. A warm pink flushed her cheeks, but she held his gaze steadily.

"Duran…" she said softly, and his name from her lips came with a sigh of longing.

"You're so beautiful." The words spilled out before his thoughts formed them.

Her lips parted, her tongue slid over them and Duran inwardly groaned. After a long moment, she whispered shakily, "I don't know what to say."

"You don't need to say anything. You are beautiful, inside and out."

Glancing away, she shook her head. "Thank you."

Behind them, the shouts and laughter of the group in the pond seemed distant. Duran gestured to the tree and without a word, she joined him to sit with their backs against it. This close, her shoulder brushing his, he could smell her light perfume, his urge to touch her becoming an ache.

Maybe this hadn't been a good idea, at least for him. Lia appeared oblivious to the effect she was having on him, smiling as she watched the play in the pond. Duran wished his body would get the message this interlude was about relaxation, not other, more tempting pursuits.

"This is great, isn't it? I mean, whoever takes time out to relax like this? It's just good for the soul, you know?"

Duran's mind was far from the soul, his or hers. "Huh?" he heard himself ask, sounding like an idiot.

Shading her eyes, she turned her face to him. "I said it's good to take time away from work, isn't it?"

"Oh, yeah, definitely."

"But it's hard to do that when there are so many pressures every day."

"Pressures. Yeah, constantly." The pressure he was feeling at the moment had nothing to do with work. Forcing himself not to stare openly at her, he focused on the boys. Maybe if he didn't look at her he could regain some inward composure because right now, red flags aside, all he wanted to do was lean in and kiss her breathless.

"Duran?"

"What?" He turned back to her. She seemed to have moved even closer, as though she'd read his thoughts and was as eager as he to accommodate them. He could kiss her now and he doubted she'd object, but wondered if they'd both regret it letting it happen.

Probably, an inner voice cautioned him. But at the moment that voice could easily be silenced if she moved a fraction closer, if her lips so much as brushed his.

He shifted, sliding his hand up her arm and she caught her breath. One slight motion and there wouldn't be any room for regrets, only feeling. He slanted his head to hers—

And in the same instant, Lia glanced toward Noah.

He knew a warning when he saw one. It shattered the sensual spell, frustrating him, but at the same time he appre-

ciated her thinking of Noah, and the possibility his son might
see them and interpret their physical closeness as much more.

She turned her face toward the endless panorama of jagged
cliffs and rugged purple peaks far beyond, avoiding his eyes.
There was nothing he could say that felt right and so he sat
with her in the shadows of the trees, in silence, wondering how
quickly things had become so complicated.

Chapter Seven

"Dr. Kerrigan's gonna be there, isn't she?"

Duran glanced up from the last e-mail he wanted to finish before he and Noah left for the afternoon. Sawyer, Tommy and Cruz's wife, Aria, all had July birthdays and in celebration, the family had decided to throw a large barbeque at the ranch, inviting—it seemed to Duran—most of Luna Hermosa. Everyone, Noah included, automatically assumed Duran and his son would be there, and Duran had made the same assumption about Lia, although no one had specifically mentioned her name.

"I don't know for sure," he told Noah, who was standing by his chair with Percy under his arm, shifting from foot to foot, impatiently waiting for an answer.

"Then call her and ask her," Noah insisted.

"I could, but it's not our party. If she didn't get invited, then I can't ask her to come."

"Why not? Don't you want her to come?"

He did, but he wasn't sure he wanted to admit that to Noah. In the course of a few weeks, she'd somehow become an important part of their lives. Lia was great with Noah. His son loved being the center of her caring attention and was quickly forming an attachment to Lia that wouldn't be easily broken. And that was fast becoming a problem.

"Dad—"

"Okay, I'll call," Duran said, avoiding answering Noah's question. "But I can't promise she'll say yes."

Lia had given him her cell number but she sounded surprised he'd used it, asking immediately if something was wrong. "I was on my way out there for the party, but I can meet you in town if there's a problem."

"There's not. One of your admirers just wanted to know if you were coming by the ranch today, but since you've answered that question, we're good."

He could almost hear her smile and with it, relax. "Well, it's nice to know I have admirers. Tell Noah I'm looking forward to seeing him."

"How about Noah's dad?" he asked.

"Him, too," she admitted softly. "I'll be there soon."

By the time she arrived, little less than an hour later, it was nearly five, most everyone else had arrived, and behind the big ranch house the talking, laughter and music signaled the party was well underway. Duran, finding himself in a group with Sawyer, his wife Maya and several of their friends from the fire department where Sawyer worked, was trying to remember all the introductions while keeping a watchful eye on Noah, playing a short distance away.

Within ten minutes of them walking into the party, his son had been drawn into a group of children around his age that included Sammy and the two Gonzalez brothers, sons of the doctor Maya worked with at the town's wellness clinic. They were all now engrossed in building various structures out of sticks and rocks for an eclectic assortment of action figures. Noah looked happy and busy and Duran thought that, if nothing else, this trip had given his son a chance to forget his problems for a while and enjoy being a kid.

"Oh, there's Lia," Maya said, pulling Duran's attention from Noah. She smiled and waved Lia in their direction. Duran found himself watching her, momentarily oblivious to everyone around him, as she made her way toward him.

She wore low-riding jeans and sandals and a tiny, deep-gold sleeveless top, and she'd left her hair loose so it framed her face, straight and smooth. She smiled for him first before greeting everyone else, the smile slipping momentarily when she recognized one of the men in the group.

"Hi, Tonio, I haven't seen you for a while."

He nodded, his return smile brief. "Likewise. How've you been?"

"Fine. Busy. How about you?"

"The same. I'm surprised to see you here, though. You've usually got some reason to be working."

The last came out with a touch of reproach and although Duran didn't understand the silent meaning behind it, the man's tone irritated him. "Today she's got some reason to be here," he said as he casually slid his arm around her waist.

The gesture had everyone looking at the two of them with mixed surprise and speculation, Maya and Sawyer in particular. Lia, a little flushed, glanced at him but didn't attempt to move away.

"I see," Tonio finally said, and might have added something else, but a woman and another couple walked up, the woman leaning into his arm as Tonio smiled down at her.

Sawyer introduced her as Rita Pérez, and the conversation turned to some planned group outing, but Duran was only half listening. He was watching Lia, her strained smile and the stiffness in her shoulders telling him she was uncomfortable with the situation. He hoped he hadn't made things worse with his impulse to defend her.

"You haven't said hi to Noah yet," he said to her. "He'll want to know you're here."

When they'd made their excuses and were out of earshot of the others, Lia stopped and turned to him. "Thanks, but you didn't have to do that. Any of it," she added.

He wanted to ask who Tonio Peña was to her and the undercurrent of animosity that ran between them, but it wasn't any of his business. Instead he said, "No, but you looked like you needed a reprieve."

"I appreciate it, but now you're going to have put up with us being the new topic of gossip around town. You've probably had more than your fair share of attention already since everyone's found out you're Jed's son. I hate being the reason you're going to get more. It's the last thing you need."

"I'll survive," he said, shrugging it off. "Besides, I'd rather be talked about for being seen with a beautiful woman than for being Jed Garrett's long lost son."

She smiled at that. "I'm still sorry. But I can't say I was disappointed to get away from that group." Hesitating, she seemed to debate with herself for a moment then sighed. "Tonio and I were—" she gestured, grasping for the right word "—together, for almost a year. It didn't end very well."

"I'm sorry. I know what that's like."

Her gaze slid away from his. "It wasn't quite the same. He's a good guy, and if I'd given him a chance, we might have…" She shook her head. "We'd been dating for a while and he wanted to move in together, to make things more permanent. I just—I didn't think it would work. He finally gave up and walked out." When she looked up at him again, her expression was regretful. "Fair warning, I'm lousy at relationships."

"My mother used to tell me people who say that just haven't found the right one." He kept his tone deliberately light, disguising the uneasiness her confession had stirred in him. She was telling him that she wasn't good at commitment and from the few things she'd said about her parents, he'd gathered that unlike him, she'd never had an example to follow, had never learned to value steadfast devotion and love. In that, she wasn't so very different from his ex, though Amber had never shown the depth of caring and concern for others that Lia did.

"If I ever found the right one, he'd be smart enough to run the opposite direction," Lia said with a short laugh, but it was layered with regrets and a touch of sorrow.

Instinctively, he wanted to reach out to her again, to offer comfort for all the past pain that had put those shadows in her eyes. She didn't let him, but, catching sight of Noah, went over to say hi, kneeling down to accept a hug and listen with apparently rapt interest as Noah and his new friends gave her a detailed explanation of their construction project.

"Noah seems to have made a lot of new friends," a voice spoke up behind him. Duran turned to find Aria and Cruz next to him. Aria nodded toward Lia, who was now examining one of Noah's action figures. "Lia's such a kid magnet. It's no wonder she's so terrific at her job." She glanced at Duran, mischief in her smile. "From what I hear, she's made an impression on you, too."

"Don't start," Cruz warned. "You're getting as bad as Maya with the matchmaking attempts."

Aria leaned back against her husband and he took her in his arms, their hands linked over the prominent curve of her belly. "Sorry," she told Duran. "I blame being pregnant. It's turned me into a sappy romantic."

"You were always a sappy romantic," Cruz murmured, brushing a kiss on her temple.

"Says you."

"When's the baby due?" Duran asked them.

"The end of August. Although with our track record, he'll probably be early or late." Aria laughed at Duran's questioning look. "So far nothing about Cruz and me has gone according to any plan, Mateo included."

"But think how bored we'd be if it did," Cruz said.

They reminded Duran of the early days of his own marriage, when life with Amber seemed almost idyllic—until the day she found out she was pregnant. Her disgust and anger with the realization quickly disillusioned him and he could only be thankful she'd cared enough about him to see the pregnancy through. Cruz was a lucky man in finding a woman who both loved him and welcomed becoming a family, even if it hadn't been planned.

He stayed talking with them a little longer, until people started moving toward the buffet tables for dinner. The three of them, he, Lia and Noah, ended up together. Lia had hesitated at first and Duran guessed she was trying to spare him new fodder for the gossips, but he knew all three of them would be disappointed if he accepted her silent offer. Instead he mouthed, *To hell with it,* over Noah's head, put aside his reservations, and let himself enjoy being with his son and her.

They talked amongst themselves, mostly listening to Noah, until about halfway through dinner, when Noah was absorbed with his hamburger and there was a lull in his chatter. Lia tilted toward Duran and murmured, "Is it me, or have you made Del's top ten list of least favorite people? She hasn't stopped glaring at you since we sat down."

Duran deliberately kept his eyes fixed on her and Noah instead of following Lia's nod to where Del and Jed sat at the end of the table. "I'm pretty sure I made number one, showing up like I did, although right now, Jed and I are fighting it out for first. Josh and I talked about it, and Jed and Del hadn't been married that long when Jed cheated on her with Lucy Miller. It's bad enough Del knows that, but from what Josh says, people in town are looking at him and me and seeing how close we are in age and coming to their own conclusions."

"Knowing Del, having people whisper behind her back is probably worse than learning Jed cheated on her," Lia said. She suddenly gave a worried frown. "Has it made things difficult for you, staying at the ranch? I feel bad, pushing you in that direction—"

"Don't. It's fine. For the most part, she avoids us, and believe it or not, Jed seems to like Noah." He laughed when she raised a skeptical brow. "It's true. He actually smiled once when Noah was telling him how much he liked going riding."

Lia started to comment, but a disturbance at the end of the table pulled their attention that direction. Del, flushed and looking on the verge of tears, had stood up and was staring at Jed with an expression that clearly said her husband had moved past Duran on her list.

"Sit down and stop your fussin', woman," Jed said, not bothering to look back. "You ain't goin' anywhere."

"We'll just see about that!" Snatching up Jed's glass, she flung the contents at him, splashing him in the face and chest, then flounced away, ignoring his sputtered curses. Josh, sitting

nearby, rolled his eyes, said something quickly to his wife and
started after his mother.

Jed half rose to follow, but Cort's hand on his shoulder
stopped him. Cort sat down next to his father, talking to him
in lowered tones. Scowling, Jed stayed put and eventually the
noise and activity of the party had left most of the crowd
oblivious to their family drama.

Shifting to look at each other, Duran could see Lia shared
his uncomfortable feeling at being witness to the exchange.
She shrugged it off, inviting him to do the same, and as one
they focused on Noah and their temporarily forgotten dinner.

Half an hour later, when they'd finished, Sammy came up
to them, wanting to show Noah a family of cats living in one
of the barns. Cort and Laurel offered to take both boys, along
with their three youngest, for a visit. Duran gave in to Noah's
pleading look, but he and Lia followed, far enough behind to
give them the illusion of being alone in the deepening
shadows of the early evening.

They could still hear the sounds of the party behind them,
but softened by the distance, and Lia let go a long breath.

"Long day?" he asked.

"Not really. I'm just glad to be away from that—" she
waved over her shoulder "—for a while." Glancing at him, she
gave an apologetic shrug. "I'm not really much of a party
person most of the time, at least not on that scale. You must
be used to it, though, living in L.A., in the business you're in."

Duran laughed. "I make documentaries, not movies, so
I'm not exactly on the A-list when it comes to Hollywood
parties. Even before I had Noah, I wasn't much into the party
scene. My ex used to say L.A. was wasted on me."

"This, at least, isn't that kind of party. Family is different."

"Well this family is a little overwhelming for me right

now," Duran admitted. "They've been great about accepting us, but they're definitely going to take some getting used to, Jed in particular."

Focusing on the path before them, a brief smile touched her mouth, a little wistful. "That's not necessarily a bad thing," she said quietly, "having so much family. They all want to get to know you and Noah and to help—well, I'm still not so sure about Jed—but your brothers, anyway."

"Aren't you close to anyone in your family?"

"Not really. I've never had much of a chance to be." She shifted her shoulders as if she carried a weight that chafed. "I've got seven brothers and sisters, but we hardly know each other. Somewhere, I've got an older stepbrother that I wouldn't recognize if we met face-to-face and I don't even have a circumstance like yours to blame. My father just never bothered introducing us."

"That seems strange. Why wouldn't he?"

"Probably because in my father's mind it didn't matter. He didn't care if all of the kids and stepkids bonded and became a family or not. He always focused on the woman he was with. Any children caught in the crossfire were left to their own devices. Neither of my parents ever encouraged any of their children to get to know each other, let alone become close."

Duran knew what he wanted to say, that people like her parents didn't deserve to have children, that the emotional scars they inflicted could be as damaging and longer lasting than physical ones. But he didn't want to put her in a position of feeling required to defend her parents, especially if her heart wasn't in it.

"I guess that's why I think it's good you and Noah have had the chance to know your family," she mused. "I know what I've missed and I hate to see someone else miss out, as well."

"I didn't know what I was missing out on until I had to go looking for them. So far it's worked out. But when it comes to Noah, I can't afford not to be careful. He's gotten very attached to a lot of people here already. I just hope it's not temporary on their part." He didn't look at her when he said it, but he could feel her eyes on him.

They were near the corral fence and she stopped, compelling him to face her head-on. "You're talking about me, aren't you?"

"Not specifically," he started, then stopped because he was lying and she knew it. "Okay, yes, I am and we both know why. Like you said before, maybe it's the circumstances, but you can't argue that Noah cares a lot about you and you and I…" He tried to find the words to define it and couldn't. "I don't know what it is, just that it's more than either of us expected."

"And apparently it's not good," she said flatly.

"I didn't say that, but maybe it's not. You're the one who told me you were lousy at relationships. Am I supposed to take the chance that doesn't apply to Noah?"

She flinched as if he'd struck her a blow in a vulnerable spot. "I would never do anything to hurt Noah. And if you believe that, we're done, not just now, but you need to find yourself a new pediatrician while you're here."

"I don't believe you'd ever do anything deliberately to hurt him," Duran said, choosing his words carefully. "But I need a guarantee you aren't going to let him learn to love you and then decide you can't deal with that or it's not what you want."

"For you or for Noah?" Momentarily confused by her snapped question, he didn't answer right away and she plunged ahead. "This guarantee, is it for you or for Noah? Because I think you're the one who wants the guarantee, Duran. And you know what? You're right—I can't give it to you. So maybe it's better we end this—whatever it is—right now."

Spinning away from him, she started back the way they'd come. Duran caught her in two paces, grasping her arm to turn her back to him. "Is that what you want? Because it sure as hell isn't what I want."

"No," she said, so softly he wasn't sure he'd heard her answer. She looked shaken and he could feel the effort she was making to hold herself stiffly, to keep her control. "But you aren't the only one who's afraid of getting hurt. I do care—a lot more than I should—and I don't even want to think about how I could hurt either of you. I don't want to think about how you could hurt me, either, when you decide it's time for you to leave. So, no, it's not what I want. But maybe it's the best thing for both of us."

She pulled herself free from his grip and quickly strode into the darkness, leaving him there alone.

Chapter Eight

Lia watched as the technician injected another needle into Sawyer's arm. "Only a little more," Lia told Sawyer. "We'll send these last samples off to Albuquerque and have the results soon. These are the last steps to making sure you're a perfect match for Noah. I don't think there will be any problems, but this is too important not to double-check."

"All done, just press this cotton ball to that spot for a few minutes," the technician instructed as she withdrew the needle. She capped the last vial, gathered up her carrying tray and turned to leave, smiling over her shoulder at Lia's thanks.

When she'd gone, Sawyer rolled down his shirtsleeve and got off the table. "So, did you have fun at the party the other night?"

"Sure, why do you ask?" Lia busied herself thumbing through Sawyer's chart and making notes.

"I don't know, it just seemed like there was some tension between you and Duran when you left."

She looked up at him. "Is Maya's emotional ESP infectious or what?"

Sawyer laughed. "I hope not. But I have to say, ever since we've been married I seem to pick up on people's moods more and more. She's like an emotional barometer for anyone who gets within three feet of her. And you know how frighteningly accurate her readings can be."

"I do know. I admit sometimes I try to keep my distance."

"I can't say I blame you. You should try living with her. Talk about feeling like cellophane. She sees right through me before I say a word."

"Yikes. I don't think I could handle that."

"Why's that? What have you got to hide?"

Lia sighed and thought about the question. She could lie to him and say nothing. Or she could tell him the truth and say just about everything. She didn't want anyone to know how her childhood, most of her past experiences with relationships for that matter, had been disastrous, leaving her terrified to believe she might actually one day be successful at one.

"That I'm a coward," she admitted finally.

"Could have fooled me. How, exactly?"

"The other night, at the party—" she began, moving to half sit on the side of the patient table. "Duran hinted at wanting to pursue some kind of *relationship* with me." Her sarcasm didn't go unnoticed. "And I shut him down."

"Why? He seems like a really good guy. And it's obvious he's interested in you."

"Maybe. And yes, he is a really good guy. Too good, as far as I'm concerned."

"I think I'm missing something here."

"He's done everything right. He had the picture-book childhood, he's raised Noah and dealt with all his medical crises alone, and he's a great father. He knows how to love someone."

"And those are bad things?"

"No, of course not. But frankly that puts his standards for what he expects out of a relationship pretty high and I don't want to put myself in a position of feeling I can't measure up."

"Is that it?" Obviously skeptical, Sawyer studied her a moment then touched her arm. "Lia, I know things didn't work out with Tonio. We have some pretty long nights at the fire station. He told me you ended it because you couldn't— or—wouldn't commit." He paused, as though giving her a moment to deny it. When she didn't, he added, "I also know it's not the first time you've done that with someone who might have made you happy. So, I don't mean to be blunt, but what's the real problem?"

Feeling suddenly exposed and entirely uncomfortable with the turn of conversation, Lia withdrew. She liked Sawyer; there had been a time, before he'd gotten involved with Maya, that they'd briefly dated. But back then, he'd been as or more skittish as her about getting seriously involved and any potential for a romantic relationship between them had led nowhere. Now she counted him as a friend but she didn't want to spill all her insecurities to him.

She slid off the table, the chart in her hand now pressed against her chest like a shield. "Some people just aren't meant for all of that—commitment, marriage, happily ever after."

"Some people don't allow themselves to find out if they're meant for it or not. I almost didn't. But look at Maya and me now."

"You and Maya are different. My family…" She shook her head.

Sawyer let out a rueful laugh. "Come on, Lia, you've met

Shem and Azure. Maya's parents aren't even in the realm of normal by anyone's definition. She grew up in a three-ring hippy circus. And Jed, my mother and my family? If you're trying to compare any issues you grew up with against my zoo of a family, we both know I win hands down."

"I wouldn't be too sure of that."

"Maybe, I don't know all that much about your family. But I gave Maya a chance and she did the same for me. Isn't it fair to Duran—and to yourself—to at least give him a chance?"

The challenge in his words penetrated her being as she turned to the door. Her back to him, she answered as casually as she could. "I'll think about it. I'm sorry but I have to go see my next patient. Be sure to drink some orange juice and have something to eat."

"Lia—"

She glanced over her shoulder, shot him an unconvincing smile. "Say hi to Maya, okay?"

She left before he could come up with another argument to convince her, her emotions and thoughts in turmoil she wouldn't be sorting out any time soon.

Because she had to, she pulled herself together, heading down the hall, rounding the corner toward the next patient room—and almost ran smack into Duran and Noah.

Great. After her disconcerting conversation with Sawyer and the way she and Duran had left things after the party, Duran was the last person she wanted to see right now. "Hi," she managed, rummaging around for a smile, for Noah's benefit more than anything. "I didn't know you had an appointment today."

"We didn't really," Duran said. "But Noah insisted on seeing you."

"About what?" Lia asked, confused. She looked between Duran and Noah.

"We're gonna visit Uncle Rafe's tribe," Noah burst in before Duran could answer. "They're gonna have a ceremony and do dances and wear strange clothes. And Dad's gonna film them."

"Really? That sounds exciting." She glanced at Duran, hoping for more of an explanation and how she fit into all this.

"I've been talking to Rafe and learning more about the Pinwa," he said. "It's his mother's tribe and they're dying out. In fact, there are only about three hundred members left. The more he tells me, the more I think it may make an excellent subject for a documentary. I've been putting off starting a new project since I finished the last one a few months ago because of everything going on. This seemed like a good opportunity to at least get started on something else while Noah and I are here in New Mexico."

"I see," Lia said, though she didn't, at least not her role in it.

"Like Noah said, Rafe invited us to visit. I'd like to take Noah up to meet Rafe's family and at the same time, I can get a better feel for the documentary possibility."

"Okay. It sounds like a great plan. What did you need me for?"

"To ask if you think Noah is stable enough to be away for a couple of days."

A fleeting thought that he might have come to invite her to go along died. There was no possibility of that; he was probably still upset with her from the party the other night. This was purely a consultation with the nearest thing Noah had to a regular doctor in Luna Hermosa.

"He'll be fine, I think," she answered with a trace of honest hesitation. When Duran frowned, she tried to sound more enthusiastic. "I mean we should go over a couple of things first, but I don't see why he should miss an opportunity like this."

Noah tugged at Duran's sleeve. "See, Dad, I told you Dr. Kerrigan would let me go." He looked to Lia, all eager anticipation. "Can you come, too? Uncle Rafe and Aunt Jule said you could."

Lia stumbled in replying. She hated to tell Noah no, but she doubted his father had any hand in his impromptu invitation. What she didn't doubt was that Jule, following her sister-in-laws' examples, was trying her hand at matchmaking and she made a mental note to tell her friend she was wasting her time.

"Rafe and Jule are both going and they're bringing the twins," Duran said, momentarily rescuing her from answering his son. "They thought you might want to get away for a couple of days. You've been burning the candle at both ends, since we got here at least, and it's a great escape from this summer heat."

His expression gave no clue as to how he felt about her coming along and Lia couldn't make sense of his even bringing up the possibility. "It sounds nice," she said at last. "Thank Rafe and Jule for me, but it's hard for me to get away. I have patients and—"

"Are you on call this weekend?"

"Well, no, but—"

Duran stepped closer, lowering his voice. "Lia, I know what we said the other night and I can't pretend that it didn't bother me or irritate the hell out of me. But I don't want to get into it now. Let's just get out of town for a couple of days, you, Noah and me. Get away from that white coat and those charts. You can't tell me you couldn't use a break. Maybe away from here, it'll be easier to figure things out."

Noah's eyes were pleading now. "It'll be so much fun. You have to go."

Lia wanted desperately to say yes. Part of her felt better about being able to keep an eye on Noah; he was so close to the transplant becoming reality, she didn't want anything to go wrong now. A larger part selfishly wanted the time together with Duran and Noah. She questioned whether they'd figure anything out, but Sawyer was right, if she never tried to forge a relationship with Duran, she'd end up with nothing but regrets for company.

"This weekend?" She was stalling and they both knew it.

"Couple of days, that's all. I'll bet you've never been there have you?"

She shook her head. Rafe's tribe was reclusive and exclusive. Outsiders only entered their land by personal invitation of a tribe member. "Actually, it sounds great. When do we leave?"

"Awesome!" Noah bounced up and down and impulsively flung his arms around her waist giving her an easy excuse to hug him back. "This is gonna be so great!"

When Duran let out a long breath, she realized how important her answer had been to him. He took her hand and gave it a squeeze. "You won't regret it. I promise."

Night dew was settling in over the scattering of ancient pine trees and desert grasses in the Pinwa village as Duran extended a hand to Lia to help her rise from the circle they'd been sitting in. Members of Rafe's tribe had just finished a beautiful dance around a bonfire. Asleep in Duran's arms, Noah lay with his head against his father's shoulder.

"He's going to be so upset he missed the ending of the dance," Duran told Lia quietly.

Lia stroked Noah's hair softly. "He had so much fun today with the other children here, he wore himself out."

Rafe, Jule on his arm, each parent carrying one sleeping twin, walked over to Duran and Lia. "You guys all set in the guesthouse?"

"We're fine, thanks," Duran answered for both of them.

"Do you think you'll be able to turn this into a documentary?" Jule asked.

"There are a lot of possibilities, from what I've been able to see so far. I'll look forward to learning more tomorrow."

"Oh, I hope you can give Rafe's tribe some help. People don't understand how hard life is for them now."

Jule's appeal for her husband's relatives touched Duran. "That's what I want to know more about."

"Plenty of time for that tomorrow," Rafe said.

After saying their good-nights, Duran and Lia walked together along the narrow moonlit path back to the little adobe house where they'd be staying.

"It feels so far away up here," Lia said, closing her eyes to breathe in the cool night air. "Mmm... Smell the pines."

Lia's own sweet scent drifted to his nose, blending with and enhancing the rich, earthy aromas enveloping them. In the moonlight the supple skin of her bare arms and short-clad legs fairly glowed. Her hair, loosened and unkempt, danced in the cooling breeze, giving her the air of a woodland nymph.

Shifting Noah in his arms, Duran reminded himself they weren't alone. They wouldn't be alone at all, even though they had agreed to staying in the same house because of the limited accommodations. In the flurry of activity marking their arrival and the day's ceremonies, neither of them had mentioned the sleeping arrangements. It was impossible not to think about it now as they walked on in silence to the guesthouse situated behind Rafe's uncle's home.

Inside Duran carefully placed Noah on a bed he was sharing with his son. Lia helped him get Noah settled by untying his shoes and easing his socks off.

"He looks so content, angelic, really," she said, gently laying a hand on the sleeping boy's cheek.

There was such tenderness in her touch that Duran felt his reservations about the whole trip fade and scatter. "I know. When he's asleep I get away with all kinds of hugs and kisses he'd never let me have in daylight." He turned to Lia. "Maybe it'll be the same for you?"

Her eyes widened then softened and she laughed quietly. "Maybe…"

Duran flicked off the light and closed the door partway. That left them facing each other, with that awkwardness he'd hoped to avoid now a very palatable third party in the room.

"It's late," she said. "I should—" She nodded toward the door of the second bedroom. She ran her tongue over her lower lip, then caught it between her teeth, the sensuous motion fixating his gaze there.

"You should," he agreed softly.

To say he didn't want to take her then and there and love her through the night would have been worse than a lie. An image of holding her, winding his fingers in her tousled hair, kissing her, with no boundaries to where he could touch her, taunted him and it took every ounce of willpower he possessed to keep from scooping her up and carrying her to that empty bed.

But to do that would be to undermine the confidence and trust in him he so wanted to give her. Unless she felt completely safe with him, she would never be able to give him, them a chance.

And he wanted that chance.

He leaned to her, gently cupping her face, and brushed a kiss against her cheek, lingering long enough for it to become a caress of breath and lips on her skin.

For a few moments they stayed like that, suspended in a place of their own making, until Lia eased back. She lightly touched his cheek. "Thank you."

NICOLE FOSTER   103

"For what?"

"For not giving up on me."

"You're making it pretty impossible."

"Am I?" She smiled a little, and there was sadness as well as wondering in it.

Duran nodded, and with an ache in his heart and one last starlit kiss, he let her go.

Chapter Nine

They were only an hour from Luna Hermosa but to Lia, after a day in the Pinwa village, it felt as if they were hundreds of miles from the pressures of reality and she decided, given the choice, it might be a good place to stay.

It had definitely been good for Duran, she thought, watching him from her corner of the room as he listened to Rafe's grandmother, Lolanne, tell him about her tribe's particular way of crafting pottery. His interest was intent and genuine; she'd never seen him so animated, excited at the possibilities of the new documentary he was already framing.

Catalina, Rafe and Jule's daughter, crawled over to Lolanne and made a grab for her beaded necklace. Rafe came to pick up the baby, but Lolanne shooed him off, setting Catalina in her lap and giving her the necklace to play with. Duran said a few words to Lolanne and Rafe, and after a quick scan of the room, spotted Lia and moved to her side.

"I see you lost your place," Lia teased.

Duran flashed a grin. "She's a lot cuter than I am."

"True, but you've got your own appeal."

"Care to elaborate on that?"

"I don't think so." The slow sweep of his gaze over her face, throat, down the skin bared by her sleeveless top touched her like a lover's caress, replacing her relaxation with a frisson of anticipation. "Not here, at least." Trying to distract them both, she indicated with a nod the living room of Pay and Mina's little house, crowded with Rafe's family. "You and Noah seemed to have gained some more relatives, in spirit at least."

"My being Rafe's brother apparently qualifies us as honorary members of the family," he said.

"And is that a good thing? For you personally, I mean." She asked the question cautiously, well aware of his reservations when it came to his son's involvement with newly acquired family and friends.

"It feels good," he admitted, "and not just because I hadn't realized how much I miss working. This place…everything seems easier. Maybe it's being away from all the drama back at the ranch."

"Maybe," she agreed softly, hoping that wasn't the only reason things seemed to much better between them.

"I think it's time I put somebody to bed."

Jolted out of her fantasies, Lia nearly—ridiculously—gave another context to his words. Instead, she followed his gaze to where Noah was sitting with three other children near Pay Nantone, Rafe's uncle, captivated by the story Pay was weaving for their benefit. Noah did appear to be drooping but mustered enough energy for an objection when Duran took him aside and announced it was bedtime.

"I wanna sleep at Yancy's house," Noah told him. "He said I could."

Duran hesitated. "I'm not sure about that. You haven't been invited by his family."

"But I want to!"

"He's welcome to stay." Kimo, Pay's oldest son, walked over, Yancy rushing ahead to add his argument to Noah's. Kimo ruffled his son's hair. "We're used to kids in the house. I don't think my wife would know what to do if there weren't at least a half dozen at all times."

"We're staying with Kimo," Rafe put in. Cradling Catalina's twin, Dakota, against his chest, he shifted the sleepy baby higher on his shoulder. "If that makes a difference."

"It's only a few doors down from yours. We were getting ready to leave ourselves," Jule added with a nod to where Catalina was practically asleep in Lolanne's arms. "It's past these guys' bedtime."

"Mine, too," Rafe said, with a look for his wife that suggested he wasn't thinking about resting.

She shook her head but smiled. "Then maybe we better go now. I can't carry all three of you."

"Can I go, Dad?" Noah begged. "Please? I really want to."

"Okay," Duran relented, "if it's all right with everyone else."

Noah and Yancy gave whoops of approval and there was a rush of good-nights, corralling the kids, and going to get the few things Noah would need for his overnight stay. Lia helped Duran get Noah settled in at Kimo's house and felt a warm rush of pleasure when Noah included her in his parting hugs as naturally as he did Duran.

"He'll be all right," she told him as they were walking back to the house where they were staying. Slanting a look his way, she tried to gauge his feelings, knowing how protective he was of Noah. "We're not far and—"

"I'm not that bad," he said, sounding amused.

"Worse," she teased back.

"Probably. It's a habit I've never been able to break."

"You say that like it's a bad thing. I wish there were more parents like you. I've seen too many children who are missing that kind of love and care."

"Like you?"

Thoughts of her own parents had crossed her mind and she laughed a little self-consciously. "It's too late for me. I'm not a child anymore."

"No," Duran said softly. "You're not. But that doesn't mean you don't still need those things."

She wanted to agree, to confess she'd been starving for them all her life. Fear held her back because admitting it exposed her vulnerabilities, left her open to a heart wound that might never be healed.

Duran stopped and she realized they were at their front door. He looked at her, then rubbed a hand over his neck, shifting to glance around them. Lia didn't want to be the one to suggest going inside. It was one thing to sleep in the same house, in separate rooms, with Noah between them, stifling temptation. It was a whole other thing to be alone together, without anyone or anything constraining their feelings or actions.

"I'm not really tired," she said quickly. "I think I'll sit outside for a while. The peacefulness makes a nice change." It was a weak excuse; she knew it and so did he.

"Do you mind some company?"

"Um, no, that's fine," she said, unable to think of any polite way to refuse him.

Neither her less than enthusiastic response nor the lack of

seating deterred him. Sitting with his back to the wall of the house, he held out a hand to steady her as she lowered herself to the ground next to him. She sat with her legs drawn up, her arms hugged around her knees. Duran's easy pose—legs stretched out, head leaned back as he studied the infinite canopy of stars above them with apparent fascination—momentarily irritated her. He seemed completely oblivious to any tension or at least content to ignore it.

She followed his gaze to where the nearly full moon spread its soft halo of light and tried to relax, to feel comfortable with the sense they were alone in the world, freed of responsibilities and worries.

The respite lasted only a few minutes, until she felt his touch, light and caressing, against her hair and it shattered any thought of finding peace.

She turned to him and found him facing her. In the shadows of the night, with only the diffusion of moonlight, she could see little. It heightened her other senses so she could hear the quickening of his breath, feel every stroke of his fingers through her hair as he loosed her confining band. She was enveloped by the scent of him, masculine and seductive.

It seemed natural and inevitable when he leaned in closer and brushed her mouth with his. He took his time, as if they had forever to learn the nuances of every feeling and sensation and to indulge in each one. It was a slow fall into a place where she succumbed to temptation and pretended there were no reasons why she shouldn't.

Her response, openly needy and wanting, broke his patience. His kisses changed from gentle exploration to intimate and urgent, as if he, too, had thrown aside any restraint when it came to what they both wanted.

And Lia did want it, wanted him, whether it was for an hour

or an eternity. Suddenly impatient, compelled to hurry and have what she could before her brain reminded her how brief and painful it would ultimately be, she slid her hands between them and started unbuttoning his shirt.

"Lia…" Her name was half groan, half plea in his husky, low voice as her fingers spread over warm skin and hard muscle. He lifted her face to his, one hand fisted in her hair, and covered her mouth with his. The sudden urgency made her feel as if they were rushing to finish something illicit.

As if he shared her thoughts, he pulled back, tracing his fingertips over her lips when she would have protested. "Not here. Come inside."

Getting to his feet, he took her hand. She let him lead her through the door of the little house, closing off the world as he shut it behind them.

A measure of sanity returned to Duran when he flicked on the lamp, the small glow of light giving him the sensation of having stepped back onto solid ground.

Then he looked at Lia, flushed and tousled, the expression in her eyes an uneasy mix of desire and uncertainty, and he felt himself balanced precariously on the edge of falling once again.

"I—" She ran her tongue over her lips, moved one hand in a helpless gesture. "Maybe this wasn't a good idea."

"Probably not," he agreed softly and immediately wished he hadn't. Pain flashed over her face and she glanced away and down. "Lia…" Feeling the loss of her warmth like an empty place had opened inside him, Duran reached out to her, gently shaping her cheek with his palm. "I want this. I want you."

With a sigh, she closed her eyes, turning slightly so her lips brushed his skin. "I want this, too, but I shouldn't." She lingered a moment longer and then abruptly broke their contact, taking a step away from him. "I'm sorry. I can imagine what you think of me right now."

"I doubt it." She expected him to be frustrated, disappointed she'd run hot and cold in the span of minutes. Part of him was—the part of him that was hard and aching for her and that insistently reminded him it had been nearly two years since he'd been with a woman. But stronger was his need to understand why she seemed determined to sabotage the start of anything that came close to emotional intimacy between them. "What are you so afraid of?"

"Of caring too much," she answered, so quietly he almost didn't hear. Like a shield, she wrapped her arms around herself. The tremulous line of her mouth betrayed her attempt to keep her voice steady. "I've lost everyone I've ever cared for, loved, in one way or another. I used to think the next time, things would be different, but they never were. If this were just sex for me, if I believed it wouldn't matter…but I can't." She put her back to him, her shoulders slumping. "I just can't."

The desire to take her in his arms, to hold her and erase every hurt and banish every ghost from the past that haunted her, surged up in him so strongly Duran had to fist his hands at his side to keep from acting on it. Her defenses were up and breaching them now by touching her might convince her he was motivated by desire alone.

He couldn't define what he felt—or didn't want to because it would mean he'd done what he'd sworn since the day Amber left him that he would never do again.

"It's not just sex," he said at last. "And it would matter."

She turned back to him, the corner of her mouth lifting slightly. "You don't have to say things you think I want to hear. I'd rather have the truth. Lies are a lot harder to live with."

"It is the truth." Unable to tolerate the distance between

them any longer, Duran closed the gap in one stride. Close enough to feel her heat, to smell the spicy musk of her perfume, he stopped short of touching her. "You aren't the only one who's lost someone they loved." Unused to sharing the darker parts of his thoughts and soul, he offered the confession reluctantly, adding, "Who's still afraid of losing someone they love."

Her eyes filled with shared pain, empathy, but there was no pity, only understanding. "I don't live with that kind of hell. Mine's of my own making. It's nothing…nothing compared with the fear of losing your child."

"Maybe not, but that doesn't make it any less real. And it's not just Noah. I'm afraid of what I feel for you. Because I'd be lying if I said I could make love to you and then tell myself that was enough, that I didn't want anything else."

Fear leapt into her eyes and she darted a look at the door as if instinctively driven to escape.

Duran couldn't stop himself taking her in his arms, holding her close despite the stiffness in her body, her resistance to the assurance he offered. "I'm not asking you for anything you can't give. I just don't want whatever this is to be over before we know what it can be."

She said nothing, but for a few moments, stopped fighting her need to be held and clung to him. There was something close to desperation in it that twisted his heart. Amber's betrayal had hurt him, left him wary of trusting in love again. Lia's upbringing, though, had caused deep and permanent scars. Where he was guarded, Lia was terrified. Yet he realized on some level he couldn't explain even to himself, the things that had hurt them most somehow were the same things that made them deeply emotionally vulnerable to each other as to no other before.

When at last she gently disengaged herself, she looked slightly embarrassed. Combing her fingers through her hair in a quick, nervous motion, she glanced at him. "It's getting late."

Sorry, I'm not letting you off that easily. "It's not that late. Sit with me for a while. Just sit, I promise," he added when she eyed him skeptically.

"Wasn't that what we were supposed to be doing outside?" she muttered. But she moved to the couch and accepted his arm around her, leaning into his side with a sigh. Idly, she started fiddling with the edges of his open shirt. "What's this?" Nudging aside his shirt where it half covered his shoulder she exposed the tattoo there, brushing her fingertips over it.

"Just a relic of my wild youth," he said lightly.

"You expect me to believe you had a wild youth?"

"Sure, it adds to my air of mystery, doesn't it?"

She made a noise that sounded suspiciously like a laugh. "I'll let you believe that. What are they?"

"*Kanji,* Japanese symbols." He covered her hand with his and guided her fingers to touch each one. "Faith. Courage. Love. I grew up believing those were the most important things in life and that I didn't need anything else. I thought they fit together, that you couldn't have one without the others. When I was young and stupid I felt compelled to advertise it via the tattoo."

"And do you still believe it?"

"Yes," he said and realized it was true, though there had been times in his past when he'd lost all three.

Tracing the symbols again, she then stretched up and lightly pressed her lips to the markings. "I want to believe it, too," she whispered against his skin.

Unwilling to risk saying anything that would cause her to bolt again, Duran simply held her against his heart and let her lean on him as she had let him lean on her when he'd needed it most.

In his head, though, he heard a small voice telling him that he wanted to be the man who convinced her it was true.

The house was still dark when slight clinking sounds and the smell of coffee woke Lia from a fitful sleep. She was alone because instead of Duran, her only companions in bed for the last hours had been memories, regrets and her fear that she had given Duran a part of herself she couldn't ever take back.

He was either a very early riser—flicking on the lamp and glancing at her watch told her it was barely past five—or he'd been wrestling with his own demons in the night and had finally given up the fight. Either way, she decided that instead of taking the coward's way out and waiting to face him until there were too many people around for it to be personal, she needed to do it now, while they were still alone.

Pulling on a pair of drawstring shorts, she went into the living area and found him slouched in a corner of the couch, dressed only in his jeans and frowning at the coffee mug in his hand.

"Is it that bad?" When his gaze jerked up, she nodded to the mug. "The coffee. You were glaring at it."

He seemed distracted by her sudden appearance, slowly appraising her from her rumpled hair down the length of her bare legs. Lia felt herself grow hot from the intensity in his gaze and wished she'd had the sense to put on something more than a camisole top and a pair of shorts.

"Was I?" he said at last. He set the mug down on the floor and stood up. "It's not that great. I'm not used to working without a coffeemaker. You're welcome to try it, but don't say I didn't warn you if it eats a hole in your mug."

"If it's the only caffeine in the house, I'll have to risk it."

The shortest path to the tiny area that served as a kitchen was passing by him; by taking the longer way around she'd make it clear she was trying to avoid him. She started around him, but he caught her arm, stopping her.

"Running again?"

"I— No."

"One thing we have in common, neither of us likes lies."

"What do you want me to say, Duran? That I woke up a changed woman? That everything's different now?"

His hold on her softened, subtly became a caress. "No, I just want you to admit there's more to us than this. And like I said before, I want to try to figure out what it is." Stubbornly keeping her near him, he ran his fingertips over her lower lip, smiling a little when she caught her breath. "Maybe we'll find it's more than either of us expected."

She wanted to agree. She wanted him to kiss her, to touch her, to make love with her until both of them collapsed. She wanted to be someone other than the woman she'd always been, the one who deliberately sabotaged every relationship she'd ever attempted.

But her own dreams terrified her. No matter how much she cared, how much she wanted to be that *other* woman, the one who could make promises and keep them, who could believe in forever, she didn't have his faith in love, or the courage to love him in return.

"I know you're scared," he said softly. "Just tell me you're willing to try."

Those were the words she longed to hear and yet—

"Duran…" Almost paralyzed by the war between her fears and her desires, Lia couldn't make herself form the words, any words, to tell him how she felt. "I—I want to. I…it's—"

Gently, he kissed her then gathered her close. "That's good enough. It'll be okay. We'll be okay. I promise."

It was a promise he shouldn't have made and she knew, in

time, when he grew frustrated with her reluctance to commit, he wouldn't be able to keep.

In his arms, though, where she wanted to be and where things felt right and certain, she could pretend to believe.

Chapter Ten

"I was thinking Tuesday evening, if that would work for you. Lia?"

She started then slanted him a guilty look. "Sorry, I missed that."

Duran frowned, keeping his eyes on the road so he didn't pass the turn to Lia's apartment. She'd been this way since this morning, distracted, withdrawn, only part of her attention on the conversations around her.

He understood, but he didn't like it. Didn't like the nagging feeling that he'd made the wrong decision when he'd told her he wanted to pursue their relationship, made a mistake in believing they could move forward.

"I was asking about dinner Tuesday evening." Pulling to a stop in her driveway, he killed the engine and glanced in the rearview mirror to check that Noah was still asleep. "Noah would love it and it would give us all some time together."

"I'll have to let you know," she said, not looking at him. "I'm on call most days this week on top of my appointment schedule."

Studying her, he let several moments tick by before he said, "Is this going to be your excuse every time? Because if it is, I'd like to know up front so I can be ready with a comeback. Don't tell me that's not what it is," he interrupted before she could say anything in refute. "You and I both know this is your idea of a preemptive strike—screw things up before they can go bad because you're so sure they will. Isn't that what happened with Tonio? You made sure you were too busy for a relationship?"

She looked at if he'd slapped her, a sheen of unshed tears in her eyes. "I don't want to talk about this now." Shoving open the door, she was out and going around the back of the SUV to get her bag before he could stop her.

Duran caught her as she was yanking up the rear hatch. "Lia, stop." He pressed his palm to the door, thwarting her attempt to get it open. "I'm not going to let you end things this way."

"Why?" she cried. The tears trailed down her face, unchecked. "You know what I am. You know I'm going to end up hurting you. Why can't you just let this go?"

"Because I care about you and I think you feel the same way about me. And I'll be damned if I'm going to let you give up on that. This time you're going to let someone love you."

Her expression stunned, she stared at him and it hit Duran that he'd all but shouted he'd fallen in love with her. Angry with her for quitting, himself for pushing things too fast, and with everyone in her past that had ever hurt her, he didn't care.

He dragged her bag out of the back of the SUV and carried it to her front door. She followed him, silent until they were standing there, facing each other—her pale and clutching her keys in a white-knuckled grip, him with his hands flexing at his sides, struggling to keep his mouth shut, afraid anything that came out of it would sound hard and frustrated.

"Thank you," she said finally. "I'll get this inside. Let me know if you need anything."

"I already have. It hasn't gotten me too far."

She flinched at his biting tone. "I meant with Noah. He's what matters most now."

"I know what you meant. I know Noah matters most. Noah will always be what matters most. But that doesn't mean this is over. Far from it." He turned and left her, not looking back, not bothering to add that despite everything that had and could go wrong, he'd meant what he said, too.

He wasn't going to let her give up this time.

"I can't do this."

Nova, heels kicked aside and curled into a corner of her office couch, eyed Lia thoughtfully as she licked the last bit of cheesecake off her fork. "What and why? Although I'm pretty sure the *what* has got something to do with Duran Forrester."

Lia stared into her wineglass. She'd come to Morente's a few minutes before closing, desperate to talk to Nova. Duran's admissions, both silent and spoken, had left her panicked, wondering how she could have so quickly lost control of the situation with him and Noah—and more importantly her feelings.

Nova had taken one look at her and hustled her into the office with a glass of wine and a huge wedge of cheesecake for each of them.

Lia watched Nova wolf down the cake. "I don't think I've ever seen you eat that much at one sitting when it didn't involve chocolate."

"Don't change the subject," Nova said, setting her empty plate down. "What happened with Duran?"

"Too much." With a sigh, Lia fiddled with the stem of her glass. "He wants—wanted—to get serious about a relationship beyond me temporarily caring for Noah. He said—" Resting her elbows on her knees, she bowed her head and rubbed at the tense cords of muscle in her neck.

"Yes?" Nova encouraged.

"Well, you know me," Lia said, not finishing because she didn't want to think about the implications of his—what? Promise? Threat? Command? "I don't do serious very well." She paused, then blurted out, "Why can't he accept that? Why doesn't he just give up and walk away?"

"You tell me." When Lia said nothing, Nova smiled knowingly. "Ah, I see."

"No, you don't."

"Come on, honey, almost anyone could figure this one out. He's serious and you're scared."

"I'm not—"

"And so you've decided to push him away."

"No—" Stopping, knowing she was lying, Lia straightened, shoving her hands through her already disheveled hair. "I don't want to push him away."

"But…?"

"But I can't trust—"

"Him or yourself?"

"Any of it, all of it. There are too many reasons for it not to last."

"Maybe you should start thinking of the reasons why it could." Nova sighed, eyeing the empty cheesecake plates with a speculative look as though considering the consequences of another slice. Then she looked at Lia and with a mischievous grin said, "I'm pregnant."

Lia blinked at the abrupt change of subject coupled with the totally unexpected announcement. "I— Wow. Congratulations."

"Since you're upset, I'll overlook your lack of enthusiasm. And before you ask, no, it wasn't planned and yes, we're happy."

"And…?" When Nova raised a brow at the question, Lia prompted, "Go ahead, give me the line about how you marrying Alex and having a baby is proof of the power of love, et cetera, et cetera."

"Please—" Nova waved her off. "You sound like a bad love song. Even if it is true," she added with a wink.

Unable to meet her friend's eyes, Lia stared down at her hands. "I'm happy for you and Alex. But it's not that simple for me."

"It could be." Nova reached over and briefly squeezed Lia's hand. "If you let it."

"That's what he said." *This time you're going to let someone love you.* "I just don't believe it. I want to but I can't, especially not this time. He's not going to stay. This isn't home for him. As soon as Noah has the transplant, he'll leave and he won't come back. I can't pretend it's going to last, no matter how serious he claims to be. And I don't need that kind of heartache, not again."

"But you want to have the courage to risk it, don't you? I know you care about him and Noah. How would you feel if after all you're going through with them, they disappeared from your life?"

"I—I can't even imagine that right now. I don't want to think about it all."

"Typical."

"I'm afraid my closeness to Duran and to Noah isn't going unnoticed around the hospital."

"You're changing the subject again. Come on, you can't

deny you're involved with Duran and his son, like it or not. If you'd just admit it to yourself, you wouldn't have to worry about trying to look professional. People will accept that you've fallen in love. But you have to accept that first."

Instinctively, Lia drew back. Denying her feelings had been her defense for so long, she didn't know any other way to protect herself.

And she had to protect herself, because otherwise, she would fall so far and so quickly, the slam into reality at the end this time would shatter her heart.

Duran stared at the papers spread in front of him, silently cursing because he'd lost his place again for the fourth time in the last ten minutes.

He'd had his lawyer e-mail the initial packet of permissions and other legal documentation he'd need to be in place before he could do any filming at the Pinwa village. In the meantime, between several commercial editing projects he'd brought with him to Luna Hermosa, he'd started the preliminary research and interviews with Rafe and his relatives. But he was having a hard time keeping his focus and found himself reading the same paragraph over again without understanding the meaning.

Finally giving up, he pushed back from the desk and went to check on Noah and Sammy. Eliana had brought Sammy over to the ranch after lunch. Duran ducked his head in the bedroom and found them sprawled on the bed.

"Who's winning?" he asked, but the boys were so engrossed in whatever game they were playing that they didn't notice him there.

He retreated again to the front room to pace, picking up papers, glancing at them, then tossing them back in a haphazard pile. He didn't know why he was bothering. It had been three days since his confrontation with Lia and all he could think about was her.

He should have known better than to push her toward something she wasn't ready for and he hated knowing she was avoiding him because of it. He didn't want to leave things the way they were between them; that was as good as admitting he was giving up. At the same time, he wasn't sure if giving up wasn't the best option. He had Noah to consider and Lia's inability to commit seriously worried him.

He eyed his cell phone and seriously considered calling her, but before he could act on his impulse, a resounding crash and the clash of raised voices interrupted. Hesitating at getting involved, Duran couldn't ignore it when another crash reverberated through the house.

Sticking his head in the bedroom door again, he told Noah and Sammy, "Hey, guys, I'll be right back, okay?"

Both boys, eyes fixed on their game, mumbled some reply Duran took as a close facsimile of "okay." He doubted he'd be missed.

The closer he got to the great room, the more it became obvious that Jed and Del were having an all-out, no-holds-barred fight. The crashing noise, Duran discovered the moment he stepped into the entryway, had come from Del flinging bottles of what looked like whiskey against the hearth. Glass was scattered in a glittering swathe over the polished wooden floor and the room reeked of alcohol.

"Stop being so stupid, woman," Jed bellowed at her.

"Oh, I will," Del shouted back. "I'm going to stop being stupid today! I'm leaving you!" She punctuated her announcement by throwing another bottle, this time at the chair nearest Jed. It cracked against wood, whiskey spattering Jed's leg.

Uncomfortable at being caught in the middle of their fight, Duran wasn't sure what he should do. Guilt pricked at him, too, coming on the heels of the feeling that part of this, at least, was his fault for showing up like he did. Jed wasn't his favorite person; he'd be lying if he said he wanted the same kind of relationship with his birth father as was starting to grow with his brothers. Yet he didn't want to be the cause of making worse whatever problems already existed between Jed and Del.

Jed, red-faced and leaning heavily on the nearest chair back, scraped his wife with a scalding glance then gave a derisive snort. "You ain't goin' anywhere and you know it."

"Yes, I am! This time I mean it."

"And where do you think you're goin'?"

"Wouldn't you like to know," Del threw back at him childishly.

She made to flounce off but Jed wouldn't let it die. "No, I wouldn't. If you're so hell-bent on leavin', then get out. But don't expect me to come runnin' after you."

For a moment, indecision crumpled Del's defiance and she wavered.

"Go on then," Jed derided. "Or have you changed your mind again?"

"Fine! But you'll be sorry. And don't expect me to come running back to you!" She nearly cannoned into Duran in her haste to stomp out of the room, giving him a furious glare as she pushed past him.

When she'd disappeared down the hallway, the fire seemed to die in Jed and he sagged, grabbing at the chair more tightly. Moved forward by the sudden show of weakness, Duran strode up and grasped Jed's arm, guiding him into the chair.

"Get me a whiskey," Jed wheezed. "In there—" He gestured to the open door on the opposite side of the great room. "If the damned woman hasn't broken every bottle."

Duran doubted it was a good idea given Jed's condition, but he went into the study and after a few minutes searching, located an unbroken bottle, poured some into a glass and took it back to Jed.

"I know our being here has caused problems for you and Del," Duran said as he watched Jed toss back the whiskey in one shot. "That wasn't my intention."

Coughing, Jed scraped the back of his hand over his mouth and leaned further into his chair. "It's been comin' on for a while now. She cares about what people are sayin'. I've had a lifetime of it and I don't give a damn. It's no one's business but mine."

"It can't be easy for her, living with all the gossip."

"She knew what she was gettin' when she married me. She was nothin' when I met her, workin' in a bar in some little nowhere town. All she was after was my name and my money. I gave her what she wanted."

Duran doubted that, doubted even more that Jed had ever given Del what she needed, but he said nothing. It made him think, though, as he left Jed a little while later to go check on Noah, about the way he'd tried to push forward his relationship with Lia.

He'd made up his mind to call her when his cell rang and he flipped it open, his pulse notching up a level when he recognized the number.

"Lia," he answered, not bothering with any greeting. "I was getting ready to call you."

"Were you?" He couldn't tell from her guarded tone if she were pleased or not.

"Yes, I've been thinking a lot about you."

There was a pause and he heard the gentle rush of her long exhaled breath, found himself holding his own in anticipation.

At last she said softly, "I've been thinking about you, too. I need to see you, Duran. It's important."

Chapter Eleven

She'd scheduled an appointment for him to see her in her office a couple of hours after they hung up the phone. Despite the stark, professional atmosphere there, she could tell he'd been expecting something personal. Instead, she'd given him more to worry about.

Lia busied herself shuffling a stack of charts on her desk, waiting for Duran to respond, bothered by his tense silence and by knowing she was responsible for it.

Across from her, he rose from the chair he'd been sitting on the edge of for the last hour listening intently as she told him she had found a transplant team that was able to take Noah right away. She'd explained to him privately what the next several weeks would hold in store for Noah and him as they readied for their trip to the transplant center at the university children's hospital in Albuquerque and the procedure itself.

Up until now, Duran had scarcely moved. At times, peering over her notes at him, she'd wondered if he were still breathing. She'd done her best to be reassuring, positive, hopeful, but the truth was there would be risks, could be complications or, at the worst, complete failure. She didn't want to downplay that aspect; it would make it all the worse if something happened.

Finally, frustration getting the best of her, she asked, "Do you have any questions?"

No response.

She waited, muscles in her neck and shoulders taut, while he stood up, paced her office for what seemed an eternity, without so much as a glance her way.

Then, so abruptly she started, he stopped in front of her. Planting his hands on her desk and leaning toward her, his eyes piercing. "You left out one important detail."

"I did?" She ruffled through her notes. "I'm sorry. What's that?"

"You didn't tell me what your part in this would be."

Baffled, Lia shoved her chair back a little, deliberately creating more space between them. "I'm not sure what you're asking. I'll follow up with Noah, of course."

"That's not what I mean."

"Then perhaps you should be more specific."

"You never said anything about coming along with us, being with Noah before, during and after the procedure."

"We've never talked about that," she shot back at him. "I thought you realized that I won't be there. Once you're at the transplant center, Noah will be in expert hands and you'll have a trained team of excellent people around you to get you through it all. This is what they do every day. It's all they do. You'll both be well taken care of."

"So—that's it then? You're finished with us?"

"I didn't say that." His attitude was beginning to irritate her, more so because this angry, aggressive stance wasn't like him. "It's understandable you're anxious, but—"

"Don't patronize me," Duran interrupted harshly. He shoved his hands through his hair, briefly turning away before swinging back to face her. "This is different and you know it. Noah is very attached to you. You can't tell me he's just another patient to you. He needs you there."

Standing, she crossed to him and met him face-to-face. "I'm not sure what you're saying, but I am sure I don't like your implications." Realizing her tone sounded sharper than she'd intended, she softened her voice. "Try to understand my position. Of course Noah is special to me, very special, but I take the best care I can of *all* my patients. In Noah's case, I can't do anything else, no matter how much I might want to. I'm not a specialist or a transplant doctor. I'm a pediatrician. I've done all I can do for Noah, at least for now."

"No, you haven't. Not if you abandon him now."

"Duran, be reasonable." Lia bit down on her own temper, knowing it wouldn't do any good to retaliate. "I'm not abandoning him. I love Noah, you know I do. And I'll stay in touch the whole time you're in Albuquerque. But I can't just drop everything here for a month or more. That's abandonment."

"I'm not feeling very reasonable right now," he muttered. "Look, Lia, I—" He stopped, blew out a breath, started again. "Noah's got it in his head that you're the key to him getting well. I've tried to convince him otherwise, but he won't listen."

She started to repeat her arguments when she realized they were all wrong. She was trying to appeal to him on a rational level and she, better than anyone, knew that logic frequently was trampled by fear.

Ignoring his scowl, she took his hand, looking straight into his eyes. "I know you're afraid but you can't control what happens from here on out."

"I need to."

"Duran—you can't. You know you can't."

"No, I—" He stopped and as suddenly as it had come, his forcefulness drained away, leaving him with an almost bewildered expression, the look of a man who'd lost his way and couldn't remember the way back. "I need to…do something."

"You are. You're supporting Noah and making sure he's got the best medical care possible."

"Noah needs you there," he said again. He paused and then added, "*I* need you there."

She wondered if it was an inborn talent that both father and son shared, the ability to put her in positions that made it nearly impossible for her to say no. It made staying professional all the harder. Though, if she were honest with herself, acting the detached professional when it came to Duran and Noah had gone out the window a long time ago.

"You're going to have a lot of support, the staff, your family…"

"I can't do this without you."

"You have been, all these years." Her heart ached until the words caught in her throat, but she forced herself to go on. "You can do this now, too. Without me if you have to."

He briefly closed his eyes and when he opened them again they were wide with anger. "Well, maybe I just don't want to do this alone anymore," he ground out. "I want you with me."

His sudden outburst shocked her; a lifetime of hiding her emotions kept her from showing it. That he had chosen her to share his emotional burdens with both frightened and awed her, moving her to give him a hope she might not be able to make a reality.

"I know it's hard to think about now, but you'll find the courage if you have to."

"Lia—at least promise me you'll try."

"I promise," she said, but reluctantly, hating that in the end she would likely have to tell him no. "I can't promise anything else but to try, though. It's too complicated. I can't give you an answer right now and I may not ever be able to give you the answer you want."

As a substitute for the reassurance he wanted, she reached out and put her arms around him to hold him, wishing it would be enough, knowing it wasn't.

"What time can you get off work today?"

Duran's voice on her cell surprised Lia. After this morning, she hadn't expected to hear from him again today, figuring he was upset with her about her not immediately agreeing to go with him to Albuquerque for the transplant. She also thought he'd want to spend as much time as possible alone with Noah. Confused, she asked, "Well, I had a cancellation, so I'll be done a little early, why?"

"Do you have a bike?"

"Well, yes, but it's got a flat tire and a bent rim. I haven't ridden in about two years. I took a nasty fall, and after walking it home three miles with a flat tire, a skinned leg and a wounded ego, I just stuck it in the garage."

"No problem. I can fix it."

"Um, thanks, but why?"

"Noah's been missing his bicycle. We left it in California because it was getting too small for him and I didn't know what the cycling situation was here in terms of trails and so on. So after this morning and with what's coming up for him, I thought a new bike might be just the thing to lift his spirits." He paused. "And mine."

"And mine?" She asked, laughing a little.

"Yes. There's nothing like a good ride to boost morale. Admittedly, I'm a cycling addict, raising a son with the same addiction, but for us it works one hundred percent of the time."

"Does Noah feel up to it?"

"Are you kidding? He's a kid with a shiny new mountain bike. He thinks he can ride straight up that cliff in our backyard. We'll take it easy, though. And it doesn't have to be a long ride. Just enough for him to get some fresh air and be a kid for a while, you know?"

"Yes, I think I do," she said around a sudden constriction in her throat. "But my bike—"

"I brought all my tools with me. Do you have a rack you can put on your car to bring it over to my place? There are some easy trails I discovered not too far from the ranch."

"I do have a rack that goes on my trunk."

"Great. Then come on by as soon as you can."

"Sounds like fun, but—"

"But what?"

Lia tried to think of a "but," but excuses failed her. "Nothing. Okay, see you soon," she told him and put down her phone, wondering at how easy it was getting to keep telling Duran yes.

Wondering what else she'd say yes to, if only he asked.

She thought again about his wanting her with him and Noah in Albuquerque, and about her reasons for hesitating, balancing them against each other. Suddenly her decision was easy.

Picking up the phone, she punched in the number of a colleague, with a new resolve to do more than try to give Duran the commitment he wanted.

* * *

Late afternoon, as the hot sun began to move toward the horizon, Duran put the finishing touches on Lia's bike. Out on the back patio of his quarters at Rancho Piñtada, Noah at his side like a surgeon's assistant handing him tools, he sat on his haunches next to her hybrid bike. He'd already pumped the repaired tire, spun the wheels to check the gears, greased the chains and tested her brakes.

"What about the fender?" Noah asked, eyeing her damaged bike critically.

Lia sat nearby on a step, smiled at the father-and-son fix-it duo. "I hit a spot with rocks and sand and slid. That was all she wrote. I still have a scar on the side of my knee. See?" Stretching out her slender leg, she pointed to her badge of courage.

Duran tried not to stare, but the cycling shorts she wore only enhanced the supple shapeliness of her legs. Noah stood and walked over to examine the scar while Duran grabbed a wrench to bend the fender back into place.

"Wow, that's cool. You must have been zooming."

"Not on purpose. I was on the downhill slope after a hard ride uphill. My speed got away from me. When I went for the brakes, it happened to be at the exact time I hit that patch of gravel. It wasn't pretty."

"But your scar is." Noah poked at it tentatively. "It's pretty awesome!"

Duran and Lia laughed. "Somehow I don't think Dr. Kerrigan sees it that way."

"Well, I didn't until now, but I think I like Noah's idea."

Lifting her bike up, Duran leaned it against the patio wall and walked over to take a closer look at the impressive scar. It gave him the perfect excuse to do what he'd wanted to do since she got there. Bending close to her, he slid one hand under her knee, the other atop the scar, brushing his palm over her leg. She didn't shy away or even flinch. Instead she seemed to be enjoying the simple touch as much as he did.

Their eyes met and she smiled knowingly. "How ugly is it?"

He traced the lighter patch of skin where the rock must have once left quite a gash. "Like Noah said, it's pretty awesome."

Ignoring them, Noah milled about nearby, checking his brakes, spinning his pedals, tuning up for the ride like a pro. "He knows a lot about bikes already," Lia said, nodding towards Noah.

"That's our thing, I guess," Duran said, standing and offering her a hand up.

The last thing he wanted to do was to stop touching her, but this was hardly the time or place. He wanted this ride to be about spending time with her, showing her how good the three of them were together.

Distracting himself, he indicated Noah. "This new bike will be good for him. He's learned to use the gears to make it easier when he needs to." He turned to his eager son. "Ready to head out?"

Noah grabbed his helmet. "I've been ready, Dad."

Lia watched Noah carefully as they rode. He'd done well, but in the last fifteen minutes had begun to breathe harder and slow down even more. They'd followed a dirt path off the ranch to a cycling and hiking trail that wound through the foothills behind the ranch. Duran had let Noah set the pace, following closely behind him and Lia. They rode very slowly, which was fine with Lia since she still felt a twinge of apprehension at the possibility of another spill into gravel, rocks, or worse, cactus.

Just as Lia was beginning to voice her concern about Noah, Duran called out to him. "Hey, Noah, let's stop a minute and have some water and a snack, then we'd better turn around. There's a good spot under that tree to the left of the trail."

Surprisingly obedient, Noah pulled off the trail, balanced his bike against the old aromatic tree and reached for his backpack.

"He's tired or he would have fought me," Duran said to her quietly, as he and Lia followed suit.

"I figured that. He was beginning to breathe hard. I'm glad you stopped."

The threesome found respective rocks to sit on, stretching arms and legs and taking in the scenery.

"This trail is different than the one at home, isn't it, Dad? It's harder."

"Yeah, that's because of the altitude and the incline here."

Noah guzzled water from his camelback. "Oh. I like the bumps and turns."

"There's definitely a lot of bumps," Lia noted, rubbing her backside. She caught Duran's eyes following the motion with interest.

"We need to get you a dual suspension bike. It'll smooth out the road for you."

We, he said we as though they were a *we.* Lia's gut reaction was to pull back, distance herself. It had been fun getting outside, riding her bike, smelling the desert earth, lavender and pine, feeling the cool mountain breeze on her bare arms and legs. And it had been really nice riding with Duran and Noah, doing something light and pleasant together.

Together was the only problem. What did that feel like to him, she wondered? Were they together as friends or more? She guessed in his mind it was the latter. And that thought made her both uncomfortable as well as curious. Was this what it felt like to be a family, doing family things, outings and such? Whatever it was it felt good. Too good. Too good to be true.

"Hey, you still with us?"

"What? Oh—sorry. I was just enjoying being outside, riding, you know, I don't get to do this very often."

"Do you always frown like that when you're enjoying the outdoors?"

Lia didn't want to make excuses or lie to him, but how could she tell him that as much as she truly was having fun with them another part of her felt out of place and ill at ease with the family-like adventure? She tried to be honest without hurting him. "I was thinking about how nice it was for you to ask me along and to fix my bike. Thanks for sharing this with me."

Looking unsatisfied with her answer, but forced to accept it for the time being, Duran studied her a moment then glanced at the horizon. "The sun is beginning to set. We need to get going. It'll be a spectacular ride back though because we'll be facing due west. We can watch the light show as the sun sets."

They gathered their helmets and zipped up their packs, each settling onto his or her bike.

As Lia looked up from adjusting her seat toward the western sky, she and Noah made similar awestruck sounds. "Oh, my gosh, look at the colors."

"And the clouds," Noah added, pointing. "Wow, they look like animals."

"Lead the way," Duran told Noah. "You can tell us what animals you see and we'll have our own spectacular painting in the sky changing before our eyes all the way home."

Lia listened to them chatter back and forth about the beauty of nature and adding her own impressions. But inwardly, as she rode along beside them, she marveled at their bond, her heart aching to be a part of it—not just in her fantasies, kept hidden in the shadows of her past, but for real, out in the light, where she could believe it would last.

Chapter Twelve

By the time they reached Rancho Piñtada, the sunset painted the very edge of the mountains, the fading reds and oranges giving way to the deeper purples and blues of twilight. Noah, Lia noticed with increasing concern, looked worn-out.

"I'll get him to bed right after dinner," Duran was saying as they took off their biking shoes and made their way into the kitchen. "You are staying, aren't you?"

"Well, I hadn't really made any plans."

"If you're worried about Jed being here, he's having dinner with Josh and Eliana. I think Eliana took pity on him because it doesn't look like Del is coming back any time soon. What surprised me more is that Jed agreed."

"It isn't that."

"You can't tell me you're not hungry." When she looked doubtful, he pointed to the cabinet. "We've kind of taken over the kitchen, in the evenings at least. I've got some great pasta sauce in there and some fresh pasta in the fridge. I can throw together a salad in minutes." Not giving her a chance to back out, he grabbed a big pot from under the stove. "If you'll just start some water boiling, I'm going to take this dusty little guy in for a quick bath."

"Don't go, Dr. Kerrigan," Noah begged. "I want to show you my new book before bed. It's about a coyote named Rattler. Isn't that funny? A coyote named after a snake?" Duran began to carry his son down the hall, Noah chattering over his shoulder all the way.

Lia's automatic flight response giving way to Duran and Noah's enthusiasm for her staying, she smiled at him, waved and turned to face the empty pot.

"You *have* to get a new bike."

Lia smiled to herself, keeping a serious face and nodding at Noah's insistence. It was the third time Noah had brought up the subject of her needing to replace what he considered her seriously lacking bicycle. Biking was obviously one of his favorite topics and he'd rallied from his earlier tiredness enough to give her all sorts of technical reasons why she needed another bicycle, comparing her bike to his new one, appealing to Duran for support of his arguments.

"I think you've convinced me," Lia said. "But I'm going to need your help in picking out a new one. You and your dad know a lot more about bikes than I do."

"We can help. Can't we, Dad?"

"Sure we can. If nothing else, we'll find you something that'll give you a smoother ride the next time we tackle that trail."

There was that *we* again, except this time, to her mild surprise, it didn't cause the familiar inward flinch. Lia marveled at how, when she allowed herself to relax, she truly enjoyed dinner and the two of them—sitting around the kitchen table, laughing and talking easily, exchanging a smile or glance with Duran now and then.

They talked a few minutes more about the various pros and cons of different styles of bicycles, and then Noah rubbed his eyes and tried unsuccessfully to stifle a wide yawn.

Duran reached over and ruffled his son's hair. "I think it's past somebody's bedtime. I'm going to tuck this big guy in," he said, rising and urging Noah up with him. "Just leave the dishes. I'll get them later. Go on out to the great room and relax. I'll be back in a few minutes."

Yawning again, Noah leaned into his father's side. "I'm kinda tired, Dr. Kerrigan. Can I show you Rattler tomorrow?"

"No problem," Lia bent and hugged him. With a light kiss to his head she smiled. "That'll give me more time to figure out his name, right?"

Noah brightened. "Yeah, it's pretty tricky. But I bet you'll get it."

She watched him head off to their wing of the house— Duran stopping once to lift Noah into his arms and carry him the rest of the way—before busying herself with the cleanup. It was easy, mindless work and it gave her a chance to reflect on the differences between her expectations for the evening— all of them awkward—and the reality, which had been so much easier, almost comfortable.

Duran came back about twenty minutes later to find her on the couch, propped against the cushions, lost in her reflections.

"Still awake?" he asked, bringing her out of her reverie. He swept an appreciative glance over her. "You look comfortable."

She gestured to the empty side of the couch. "Sit down, you must be exhausted."

"Getting there," he admitted lowering himself next to her.

Looking over at her, he reached for her hand, twining their fingers together. "Are you okay?"

"I'm fine. Why?"

"Earlier, you seemed—" she sensed him choosing his words carefully "—uncomfortable with the whole idea of staying for dinner."

"I was." Hesitating, she added, "I've never really done this, the things that normal families do. It doesn't feel real to me."

"I hate to ask what does."

"I was thinking about that." She dropped her head back against the cushions, following with her eyes the patterns in the heavy wooden beams of the ceiling. "When I was growing up, if we had dinners as a family, it was usually at a restaurant, and there were other friends or my father's colleagues around, so we didn't have to actually talk to each other. Otherwise, if we were at home, it was pretty much everyone for himself. I can't remember ever sitting down with both my parents and my brothers or sisters and having dinner together, or any other meal for that matter. It was nothing like how you are with Noah."

She turned to look at him and found him watching her, a slight frown between his eyes. "It's hard for me to imagine that as it much be for you to imagine what it was like for me growing up." He shook his head. "I never want that kind of life for Noah."

"There's no chance of that. If either of my parents had been half the parent you are—" There was nothing else to add because there was no comparison.

Duran stroked his thumb over the back of her hand, the motion an offer of understanding and assurance. "It doesn't mean you can't have what normal families, as you call them, have. It's never too late."

"I'd like to believe that."

"But…"

"It's hard," she admitted. She thought about the day and how very domestic it all felt, the three of them being together. It hadn't seemed as difficult as she'd imagined it would. "Maybe I just make it hard."

"Sometimes," he agreed. "Maybe it's your self-defense."

"I guess. Whatever it is, it's not an easy habit to break."

"I can understand that. "I've got a few of those bad habits myself."

"Because of Noah."

"Because sometimes I make things harder than they should be, too," he countered. "Yes, I've got Noah to think about. I'd do anything to keep him from getting emotionally involved. I wasn't going to put myself in the position of caring for someone and then risk having her walk out when things got tough. I didn't think it was worth it."

His use of the past tense raised questions she didn't ask. But it made her wonder of his change of heart had been influenced by his reunion with his family and their acceptance of him and Noah, or if she, in some way, had been the cause.

The idea was both daunting and seductive in equal measure. Putting it aside, she focused on Duran. He looked tired as he rolled his shoulders, the motions still and slow.

"Noah's not the only one who needs an early bedtime," she said. Sliding closer to him, she reached over and began gently massaging the muscles in his neck and shoulders.

Duran closed his eyes and lightly pressed into her touch. "Probably. It was worth it, though. Noah loves the new bike."

Unable to resist, she leaned over and kissed him. "Thank you for including me. It meant a lot to me."

"It meant a lot to us, too," he said, and she could see the truth in his eyes. "See, it wasn't as bad as you thought it would be."

"Not bad at all. I might have even liked it—a little."

"Now that—" his arms slipped around her and she found herself facing him, sliding her hands around his neck "—sounds like a challenge. What can I do to make it a lot?"

"Well…" she mused, pretending to think it over when all she wanted to do was kiss him again. "Dessert would be good, if it's chocolate."

Shifting closer, he nuzzled her cheek, his mouth grazing her skin. "I have a confession to make. I hate chocolate."

"Oh, well, then it's definitely over between us. I could never consider being with a man who hates chocolate." She said it even as she lifted her chin to give him better access to her throat. The last word came out with a low hum of pleasure.

"I like white chocolate," he murmured, his breath warm against her ear.

"Sorry, that doesn't count. It's the good stuff or nothing."

His hands wandered, and hers wove into his hair. "I've got some good stuff," he said.

"I'll have to decide that for myself."

She kissed him then and he kissed back, his soft and sensual caresses quickly becoming deeper and more intimate. Instead of satisfying, though, the taste and feel of him on her mouth and body only intensified her growing ache for more.

It wasn't enough. She wanted more, and yet she couldn't forget that Jed would be home soon and Noah was only a hallway apart from them. That Duran shared her conflicted feelings was evident when, with a frustrated groan, he pulled back far enough to rest his forehead against hers.

"This probably isn't the best idea here and now," he said.

"I know." Making things more difficult, Lia quickly kissed him, then repented and put a few more inches between them. "I should go."

"You should," he agreed even as he closed the distance again and claimed another kiss.

It was another fifteen minutes before they finally, but reluctantly, moved off the couch. Lia retrieved her bag and shoes, and Duran followed her to the door. She paused there, catching her lower lip in her teeth for a moment, before deciding to tell him something she hadn't intended on revealing this evening.

"I'm working on my schedule so I can go with you and Noah to Albuquerque, at least for the transplant procedure and that first week or so of recovery. Those first few weeks will be the hardest."

She caught him without a reply. Surprise and a little confusion flashed over his face and he looked as if he wanted to say something but stopped himself and only nodded.

Lia knew she hadn't given voice to her feelings or spoken her commitment to him and Noah and any future beyond the short-term. But in her own way she was telling him that deciding to go to Albuquerque with them meant she wanted to try, and she hoped he could hear what she couldn't say.

Slowly he drew her to him and she softened, sliding her arms around him as he held her against his heart. "Whatever happens, I'm ready to face it." He touched his lips to her forehead. "As long as you're there."

Instead of fear, she felt grateful that he needed her and trusted her that much.

Though the voices that had always haunted her chided her still, telling her Duran held unrealistic ideals about love and family she couldn't believe in, ones that in the long run would fade away and die in the face of reality, and that she had no experience with commitment, a new, small voice in her heart began to take root.

It was a whisper, not strong enough to be a certainty, but it encouraged her to trust that with him, it might not have to be that way. It could be different. She could be different.

With Duran's faith in her, maybe the past didn't have to poison the possibilities of the future.

Chapter Thirteen

"This is all my fault."

Duran had been prepared to face the challenges of the transplant. But he wasn't prepared for this.

Lia, bent over to recheck Noah's IV, glanced over at Duran. "No, it isn't," she said quietly. Smoothing damp strands of hair from the little boy's face, she gave him a lingering once-over before moving to where Duran stood at the foot of Noah's bed. She touched his hand. "Let's go outside for a few minutes. He's asleep and we'll be able to hear if he needs anything."

Although reluctant to leave his son, Duran complied with her gentle prodding. Once outside, he linked his hands behind his neck, closing his eyes and leaning his head into his palms to try to ease the ache of tension that stretched from his head down his spine.

"Do you want some coffee?" Lia asked.

Duran shook his head. "No, thanks." He took in her disheveled appearance—the hastily tied back hair, jeans and slightly creased shirt, and lack of makeup—knew he didn't look any better. "But don't let me stop you."

"I'm fine. And Noah will be, too. Just give the antibiotics a chance to work."

Blowing out a long breath, Duran tried to believe that. It had only been a few hours since she'd left Rancho Pintada and they'd parted with promises to talk again tomorrow. Only tomorrow had come a lot sooner than he'd anticipated. Shortly past midnight, Noah had awakened complaining that he felt sick and his head hurt. When the thermometer revealed a one-hundred-four fever, Duran had wasted no time in calling Lia and she'd beat him to the hospital emergency room by ten minutes.

Noah's infection was serious enough that Lia again had him admitted and started him on intravenous antibiotics. Now, two hours later, Noah was sleeping, and the guilt that had visited Duran when he first discovered his son was sick again came back to hit him with a vengeance.

"If I'd been taking better care of him, he wouldn't be here," he said. He briefly covered his eyes with his hand, squeezing hard. "I let him do too much—especially the bike ride. He wasn't ready for that. I should have known this would happen."

"Stop it," Lia said and the sharpness of her tone brought Duran's head up. "Your wallow in guilt isn't helping. Noah's much better off for having been able to spend time with his family and make new friends. You know as well as I do that his mental attitude is more than half the battle when it comes to his recovery chances." She gentled her stance, moving close to slide her hand against his jaw, ensuring he looked into her eyes. "You've made all the right decisions for Noah and more importantly, you love him. That's what will get him through this and everything else to come."

"When did you become such a believer in the power of love?" Duran asked with a slight smile.

"There's this stubborn guy who keeps telling me it's true. Now it's time for him to prove he really does believe it, too." She stretched up and lightly kissed him. "He'll be okay," she vowed. "I'll do everything I can to make sure of it."

"I know you will. Lia, I—"

Lia held up her hands. "Please don't thank me again. It's completely unnecessary. I love Noah, too. I'm not doing this to gain your eternal gratitude."

He knew she wasn't but when she left for a few minutes to talk to the night nurses, Duran wondered if he was letting his gratefulness get in the way of his clarity. He cared deeply about her but as he watched his sleeping son he wondered how much he could attribute this to the compassion she showed Noah and him in so many ways.

It was just past six, Noah was still sleeping and Duran had taken a break from his bedside vigil to stretch his legs in the hallway when Sawyer rounded the corner carrying a large travel mug and a cloth shopping bag. He was in uniform and smiled at Duran's questioning look.

"Jed found the note you left and for some reason I can't yet explain, he called me," Sawyer said. "My shift starts at seven so I thought I'd swing by first and bring you some coffee. Maya sent muffins, too, although I gotta warn you, her specialty is organic weeds and sticks."

"Thanks," Duran said, accepting the mug and bag. "I definitely appreciate the caffeine. It's been a long night."

"How's Noah?" Sawyer asked.

"His temperature's still up but it's not as bad as it was. Lia thinks a day or two of intravenous antibiotics will kick the infection. She ran home to grab a shower but she should be back soon to check on him." Setting the bag down next to him, Duran leaned his shoulders against the wall and took a long drink of the coffee, welcoming the buzz from the strong brew.

"Is this going to delay the transplant?"

"It depends," Duran said. "If Noah can shake this quickly, it won't matter. If not, we'll be putting it off for a week or two."

Sawyer nodded, then hesitated for a moment before asking, "Is Lia going with you to Albuquerque?"

At first, Duran balked at answering, knowing how much it would reveal about his feelings and hers. "Yes, she's planning to," he said finally.

"That's good—isn't it?"

"I don't know. I thought it was." Duran blew out a breath. He wasn't yet used to having brothers he could use for sounding boards, but maybe saying out loud the things going through his head would help sort out his feelings. "I care about her. Actually, I'm pretty sure it's a lot more than that, but I don't know how much of it is because of everything we've been through with Noah. She's been so understanding and supportive, sometimes I wonder what I did without her all this time."

Sawyer didn't comment, yet his brother's silence was encouraging in itself.

Pushing a hand through his hair, Duran stared at the opposite wall. "I don't understand why I let this happen this fast. After Amber left me, I swore I wouldn't get seriously involved again, especially with someone like Lia. She's terrified of commitment. She doesn't believe anything lasts—just the kind of woman I should be avoiding like the plague."

"It sounds to me like you're trying to talk yourself out of loving her," Sawyer said.

"Maybe I am. I don't want to push her out of my life but

I'm worried about what could happen if, down the road, she decides it's not worth the risk. If it were only me—but I've got Noah to think about."

"I don't have any answers for you. You're the only one who can decide whether or not it's worth the risk for you. It would definitely be easier to give up and move on rather than take the chance."

There was no reproach in Sawyer's tone, just a blunt assessment of the situation that Duran agreed with. Yet his fears for his son, intensified now with this latest crisis, were clouding his ability to think straight when it came to his feelings for Lia. He'd come to depend on her support; he needed her more than he was willing to admit. And he was afraid that would lead him to make the wrong choices, bad decisions that could leave permanent scars.

Sawyer was right—it would be easier to give up, turn his back on the equal chance of love and heartache. If he did that, he might be protecting his son from being hurt, but he would also be showing Noah by his own example that he didn't really believe that love was worth the risk. And it would make a lie out of every argument he'd used to convince Lia to take a chance on them.

How could he ask her to open her heart when he wasn't willing to do the same?

Lia made the last notation on her long list with a flourish, smiling at herself. It had meant making a lot of tedious notes about patients, rescheduling and calling in a favor or two, but she'd managed to organize things well enough so she could leave with Duran and Noah with a clear conscience. Her other patients would be well taken care of in her absence.

Strangely, instead of finding the prospect of going daunting, she felt good. She had, in a way, made a commitment to him and surprisingly, she hadn't been struck by lightning or attacked by paralyzing panic. She still wasn't ready to admit everything she felt for him but she was taking the first step toward overcoming her fears.

With a final pat to her calendar, she decided to check on Noah. She'd tried to spend as much time as possible with him and Duran the past few days, keeping a close watch on Noah's recovery and encouraging Duran to get out of the hospital long enough to change clothes, sleep and eat. He hadn't liked it but he'd grudgingly complied for short periods and with that she had to be satisfied.

It was past dinner and she expected to find Duran in his usual post by Noah's bed but Noah was alone. Sitting propped against the pillows, Percy tucked against his side, he was studying a book with a slight concentrated frown.

"Hi, there," Lia said, answering Noah's sudden smile with one of her own. "You look like you're feeling better." She touched her fingers to his forehead, pleased to find he felt only slightly warm. Quickly, she scanned his chart and saw his last temperature reading, an hour earlier, was barely one hundred.

"I'm okay," Noah muttered. "I wanna get out of here. I hate this thing." He jabbed a finger at the IV still attached to his left hand.

Lia sat on the edge of the bed. "I don't blame you. But it has to stay for at least another day. Then, if your temperature stays down, we'll see about taking it out and letting you go home. Deal?"

"I guess."

"So," she said, trying to distract him, "where's your dad?"

"He had to call somebody about work or somethin'. He said when he got back he would read me this." Noah held up the book and Lia guessed from the dragon and boy depicted on the cover it was some sort of fantasy story. "I was trying to read it to Percy but there's lots of words I don't know."

He eyed her hopefully and Lia hid a smile. "Well, I'm probably not as good a reader as your dad, but I could give it a try while we wait for him."

"Dad always sits next to me," Noah pointed out when Lia took the proffered book. "Sit here—" He scooted over to give her space and she obliged him, feeling a warm happiness settle inside her. Noah hugged Percy close and rested his cheek on her shoulder as she started to read.

Over half an hour and a chapter later, the door pushed open and Duran strode in, pulling up short, his smiled greeting dimming when he realized Noah wasn't alone. "I guess I shouldn't have worried about you being by yourself," he said, coming over to stroke Noah's messy hair. "You guys look comfortable."

"We're readin' the dragon book. Dr. Kerrigan likes dragons, too." Noah yawned and both Duran and Lia smiled.

"Looks like it's bedtime," Duran said.

"I'm not tired," Noah insisted. "Can we read just a little more? Pleeease, Dad?"

Duran exchanged a glance with Lia over Noah's head. She shrugged a little to indicate it was up to him. "Okay, ten more minutes. But only if you promise not to complain when I say it's time to stop and get some sleep."

Nodding happily, Noah settled back into his place against Lia's side, and, a bit self-consciously with Duran looking on, she resumed the story. By the time the allotted ten minutes were up, Noah's eyes were closing and he didn't make any protest as Duran helped him get ready for bed and then tucked him in with Percy. Noah insisted on a hug from both his father and Lia, and then snuggled under the blanket.

Ten minutes later, when Noah was fully asleep, Lia accepted Duran's silent invitation to step outside the room.

"Thanks for being my stand-in," he said but without an accompanying smile and with an edge to his voice Lia didn't fully understand.

"Stand-in only, not a replacement. I was second choice, believe me. I just happened to be handy."

Duran rubbed a hand over his face. "I'm sorry, I'm pretty sure I just sounded like a jealous, overprotective jerk."

"That's a little harsh," Lia said. She tilted her head to one side, considering. "You're definitely not a jerk."

"Guess I'll have to work on the other."

"Guess you need to get some sleep and I don't mean those naps you've been taking in that sad excuse for a chair in there," she said, pointing toward Noah's room. Reaching out, she curled her fingers around his for a brief moment. "Noah's much better. In a day or two, he'll be able to leave and then you can get ready for Albuquerque. Save your worrying for then."

"I notice you didn't tell me not to worry," he said.

"I'm not going to bother wasting my breath." Lia hesitated, then asked, "Is it still okay if I go with you?" His shuttered expression didn't give her confidence that it was what he wanted anymore and, wounded, she nearly backtracked, and told him to never mind, that she'd stay here and let him do this on his own.

"It's okay," he said finally. Before she could question his sincerity, Duran pulled her into his arms, holding her tightly. "It's more than okay. I appreciate it more than you know, for Noah's sake. This is what he needs to give him the best shot at getting through this."

His less than whole-hearted reply tempered her happiness with a shadow of doubt.

She couldn't deny his lackluster response hurt, but Lia couldn't regret her decision, and chalked his doubt up to stress and fear for Noah. She chose to simply enjoy being in his arms, and in a corner of her heart she prayed that this time, as she dared to risk falling in love, love would not betray her.

Chapter Fourteen

"Are you sure you feel okay?" Duran held Noah's hand as they walked slowly from their rooms to the great room. The rest of the family had already gathered there to celebrate the latest addition to the clan, Aria and Cruz's new son Mateo.

Noah's expression asked if his dad was kidding or just plain stupid. "I'm fine. I want to see my cousins. I'm sick of being in bed. It's boring."

"Okay, we'll go for a while, on one condition."

Noah puffed out an exaggerated sigh. "What?"

"That when I say it's time for a rest, you don't give me any lip about it."

"Okay, okay."

The sounds of now familiar voices and laughter grew louder as they moved into the great room. Duran still couldn't believe how many relatives he had and at times it was diffi-cult to accept he was a part of Jed Garrett's family. But having all these cousins, uncles, aunts and even a grandfather of sorts around him had proved to be some of the best medicine Noah could take.

They walked into the room, usually so large and empty the sound of two voices was merely an echo. But with all of the children scampering around, squealing, playing while their parents talked with each other, the room felt crowded.

"Hey, Noah," Tommy called from across the room. "Come here. I got that new game I was telling you about."

Noah tried to pull his hand from Duran's to take off toward Tommy. Duran gripped a little, keeping him in place a moment longer. "Slow down there, remember what Dr. Kerrigan said?"

"I know, Dad. You already told me like ten times now. Can I go?"

Duran released Noah's hand and watched as his son tried to contain his eagerness, forcing himself to walk instead of run. He hated to have to temper Noah's natural exuberance, but if Noah didn't get his strength back, they'd have to postpone the transplant again.

"How's he doing?" Rafe's deep voice sounded behind Duran. He turned to see his brother eyeing Noah with concern.

"Better, thanks. It's hard to keep him calm when he's so happy to see everyone."

Cort made his way to join the twosome. "Hi," he said, shaking Duran's hand. "I told Tommy to take things easy today and I know Josh and Eliana gave Sammy the same message. But if they start to get rowdy, one of us will put a stop to it."

"Thanks. I know I keep saying this, but I do appreciate everything all of you have done for us."

"We're family." Rafe put a hand on Duran's shoulder and

smiled. Something Duran rarely saw his brother manage, but when he did, it was genuine and straightforward. "Just because you're new to it doesn't mean you don't belong."

"You weren't going to add 'whether you like it or not,' were you?" Cort teased his older brother, earning him an expression between rolled eyes and amusement. "Speaking of like it or not—" He nudged Duran's arm. "The old man is trying to get your attention."

Duran glanced over to where Jed sat in his oversize leather chair. Cigar in hand, he motioned Duran over to him. "He's looking worse," Duran commented, noting Jed's pasty complexion and the way the cigar trembled in his hand.

"Yeah, well," Rafe said with a derisive snort, "according to Jed, nothing a cigar and a couple of shots won't cure."

"I'd better get over there before he tries to come after me," Duran said. "He's not been getting around too well lately." He glanced at Noah, who sat on a big Navaho rug playing a video game with the other boys, ensuring his son was happily occupied, and then excused himself and made his way to Jed.

"Thanks for asking Noah and me to join you today," he said.

Jed grunted. "Thank your brother. It was Cruz's idea to have this circus. He wanted to show off that new boy of his to everyone. My boys are breedin' like rabbits." With a wave of his hand, he gestured Duran to sit. "Tell me, how's your boy doin'?"

"He's better. If everything goes okay, we'll be leaving next week for Albuquerque and then we'll be staying there for at least a month, maybe longer depending on how Noah does with the transplant."

"You sure he's up to it?" Jed asked, narrowing his eyes to assess Noah. "Not much to him these days."

It was the warmest show of concern Jed had mustered

since they'd arrived in Luna Hermosa and Duran realized it was probably the closest Jed ever got to compassionate. "He's lost a little weight but as long as he takes it slow and gets enough rest, he should be ready."

He paused as Jed downed another whiskey shot. He, too had lost weight and looked even older than he had when Duran first arrived. But the muscles in Jed's forearms below his rolled up shirtsleeves still flexed with a power men half his age hadn't achieved. The old man was built of steel, reminding him of a mountain man or trailblazer from a century past; reminding Duran again of his twin, both in stature and temperament.

"How are you feeling?" he asked, sure he'd get little more than a brush-off in return.

"Old and mean," Jed scoffed, reaching for his bottle to pour himself more whiskey. "Same as I've felt for the last thirty years. And now that that damned woman has run off and left me with some stranger to fix my dinner, I'm feelin' even meaner."

Behind him Duran heard a round of oohs and ahs and turned to see that Cruz and Aria had arrived with their son and were already enveloped by the crowd of eager siblings, in-laws and cousins.

Jed shook his head at the fuss over the new baby. "If my boys keep havin' kids, pretty soon we're gonna have enough of this family to start our own town." Although it was gruffly spoken, there was a note of pride in Jed's voice, as if he judged his own success by the size of his family. He turned back to Duran. "You got yourself a rough road ahead of you. You and that boy of yours."

"Maybe, but we'll be okay. We've got your genes, after all."

"Best thing I ever gave you," Jed said, his short laugh turning at the end to a croaking cough.

"I think so," Duran said and couldn't help a smile. "I'll

catch up with you later. I'm going to take a look at your newest grandson."

"You do that. Tell Cruz I want a look at him myself, when all those women are through makin' a fuss over him."

Jed Garrett was something else, Duran thought as he moved over to the group gathered around Cruz and Aria. Jed wasn't the easiest of men to like or even respect and Duran didn't know if he'd ever be able to accept him as a father. But he'd passed his gutsy strength and stubborn determination on to his sons. And right now, that was something Duran needed more than anything to get through the weeks to come.

Jule and Eliana stepped aside as Duran approached. "He's precious, just precious," Jule was saying. "Hey, Duran, come take a look at our new nephew." Jule waved him in front of them.

Aria held the tiny swaddled baby, Cruz beaming proudly over her shoulder. Mateo slept peacefully in her arms, oblivious to the multitude of admirers.

Duran took in the baby's face, olive-skinned with a shock of jet-black hair on his tiny head. He remembered Noah being that small and fragile, angelic in his perfection. If only he could have known sooner that a devil of a disease would invade his son's body, if only he could have caught it sooner, prevented it all together...

"He's perfect," a soft voice, familiar in its understanding and gentleness, spoke the words Duran found hard to form just then. He looked up from Mateo to see Lia across from him, watching him, her smile tempered by concern, as if to let him know she knew how much he was struggling with the moment.

He smiled back and the constriction in his throat eased.

Aria, rocking her son in her arms, beamed up at him. "Thanks, we think so, too."

"I don't want to interrupt our group admiration of this little guy," Maya raised her voice above the hum of conversation. She bent down to scoop up her and Sawyer's youngest son, Nico, when the toddler tugged at her skirt. "But there's a buffet set up in the dining room. We're going casual tonight, so go grab what looks good whenever you're hungry."

As the group began to disperse, Lia moved to his side. Duran touched her hand. "I didn't know you'd be here tonight, but I'm glad you are."

"Maya called earlier and insisted I come. I hope I'm not intruding."

"Of course you aren't. You're practically family," Maya, coming up to them, said before Duran could answer. "You're our family pediatrician after all. These little munchkins are all your babies, too."

Lia glanced over to Mateo, now cuddled in Cruz's arms. "They feel like it." Her smile was a little wistful. "And that Mateo, he was so stubborn. He had no intention of being on time. I have a feeling that little boy is going to be quite a challenge."

"All the boys and men in this family are," Maya said, with a mischievous grin. "Speaking of that," she said craning her neck to eye her older son Joey. "I think I'd better go run interference before Joey and Sophie have a war over who gets the red blocks."

Alone again with Lia, Duran knew he owed her an explanation for his reticence. But how could he explain what he'd been thinking without hurting her? That, no matter how deeply he felt for her, even loved her, frankly, a lot about her, about her past, scared him.

"Are you okay?" Lia asked, the brush of her fingers on his shoulder pulling him out of his thoughts.

"Sure, fine. I'm still not used to all the big family gatherings. It feels a bit overwhelming sometimes."

"Believe me, I understand. But—"

"But what?"

She broke eye contact with him and glanced off, a small smile playing with her mouth. "It's kind of nice, isn't it? I mean look at them all. They've been through so much in this family and yet they're united for each other." She looked back at him. "And for you and Noah. That's pretty amazing."

"I know. I'm feeling pretty amazed and lucky these days." He paused then told her, "The family circle is going to get bigger tomorrow. My parents are coming in from Rio Rancho to see Noah and to meet everyone," he said in reply to her unspoken question. "I'd like you to meet them, too."

Uncertainty flashed into her eyes. "Are you sure?"

"Yes. Noah's told them all about you. They're anxious to get to know you."

"Ah, well—I wouldn't want to disappoint Noah."

"I want them to get to know you, too. You've done so much—"

"It's my job," she interrupted shortly. "The transplant staff is going to do more than I've been able to."

This was going badly, twisted by her insecurities and his doubts. Duran tried again. "It's not about doing your job. I want you to meet them because you're important to me. Have dinner with us tomorrow night. Cort and Laurel are going to take care of Noah and Cort made reservations for us at Morente's. I told him there'd be four of us."

"I don't know if it's such a good idea. You've been—"

"I want you to be there. Say yes."

She hesitated and then nodded, although she didn't appear entirely convinced it was the right choice. Her glance slanted away from him and something caught her eye. "Duran—look at that."

Duran followed her line of sight and they both stared.

Someone had pulled up a footstool for Noah to sit on next to Jed. Perched on the edge of the stool, Noah leaned toward Jed, grinning ear to ear, apparently captivated by some story Jed was telling him. Jed also leaned toward Noah, arms and hands animated, cigar waving between his fingers, as he spun some yarn to his grandson's utter amazement.

"We ought to get a photo," Lia said. "Because I'm pretty sure it's the first time anyone has ever seen anything like it." She leaned closer while they watched Noah and his grandfather and asked, "Has Noah's appetite picked up? He still looks a little peaked."

"It's better. He grumbles sometimes, but I think he's doing what I ask as much to please you as anything."

"Oh, I doubt that." She shrugged and shifted away from Duran. "But whatever works at this point. You don't want to have to postpone this any longer than necessary."

"No, we don't," he agreed, slightly emphasizing the *we*. Brushing his palm down her arm, he took her hand in his. "Lia, listen, I'm sorry if I didn't sound exactly thrilled the other day when you told me you were coming with us. I've just got a lot on my mind. I want you there. Noah wants you there. I hope you know that."

"Hey, you two, food's getting cold," Eliana called to them from the hallway.

Lia waved and nodded. She raised her eyes to his and for a long moment, held his gaze steadily, searching as if for some truth he hadn't given her. "I know," she said finally. Avoiding his eyes, she slipped her hand from his. "We'd better go join the others. I'll get a plate for Noah. I'd hate to pry him away from Jed. This may never happen again."

"We'll talk more later, okay?"

"Of course, if that's what you want."

Her distance frustrated him and at the same time, left him angry with himself for mishandling the situation. He should have been completely honest with her. She knew him well enough to know he hadn't been.

But how could he tell her that although he believed she loved him, and he had fallen in love with her, he was afraid her love might not be strong enough to build a future on?

The rest of the night was pure hell.

Lia choked down a few bites then made excuses about evening rounds at the hospital, beating a hasty exit from Rancho Piñtada but mostly from Duran. Ever since she'd told him she would go with him and Noah to Albuquerque he'd acted strangely withdrawn. After the party, she'd spent a sleepless night trying to understand his apparent change of heart.

Was it her or him? None of it made sense.

No, what didn't make sense was this. She looked at herself in her mirror, at the skirt and shirt in tones of gold she'd chosen and wondered what the heck she was doing.

She wished now she'd turned down his invitation to have dinner with his parents. It had seemed like a bad idea at the time, doubly so now.

Doubts beset her. She wondered exactly what Duran had told them about her. Maybe it was better if he'd said she was nothing more than his son's temporary doctor and a friend. But that bothered her because it was a poor description of their relationship, even though neither of them seemed inclined to define exactly what that relationship was.

Too many questions with no answers were about to drive her over the edge. Forcing herself to think about anything else, she stepped into a pair of cute slingback sandals and smoothed her hair.

"This will have to do, good enough or not," she said aloud to her reflection and grabbed her car keys.

Duran apparently thought it was more than good enough, if the appreciative once-over he gave her when they met outside Morente's was any indication. Surprising her, he slipped a hand around her waist and lightly kissed her hello before introducing her to his parents. "Mom, Dad, this is Lia Kerrigan. Lia, I'd like you to meet my mom, Eliza, and my dad, Luke Forrester."

"It's a pleasure to meet you," Lia said, extending a hand to the comfortably conservative looking couple. They were considerably older than she'd expected and she guessed they'd been in their forties when they'd adopted Duran.

With a tremulous smile, Eliza gripped Lia's hand between her palms. "Noah can't stop talking about you. You can't imagine—" Her voice broke and her husband wrapped an arm around her shoulders. She glanced up to him and he smiled down at her.

"What my wife is trying to say is thank you. We've been praying for a miracle. And you might just be the one to make that miracle happen. We can't thank you enough for all of your time and caring for our grandson."

"No thanks necessary, Noah's very special to me, too," she said. "We were lucky Sawyer was a match. I had nothing to do with that."

"Duran's been lucky to find his brothers. They've been wonderful, too," Eliza said. "Of course we were quite taken aback at first but after meeting all of them we're delighted for Duran and Noah. We're hoping to get to know Ry better, too. All family is good family."

Lia begged to argue that point but held back. That was precisely the subject she didn't want to bring up. She looked to

Duran and wondered if it was inevitable that he'd make comparisons between the abandonments and failed relationships in her life, and the constants, love and tradition in his.

She couldn't do this. How could she ever give this man what he needed, be the woman he wanted?

As Duran let his parents lead the way into the dining room, he turned to her. "You're upset," he said flatly.

"No, I'm fine."

He dismissed her protest. "I don't know what you're thinking but I can see whatever it is isn't good. I'm sorry we haven't had any time to talk. I know things are building up that we haven't been able to deal with. But please, don't shut me out."

"I should be saying the same to you."

"I know." He dragged the backs of his knuckles gently down her cheek. "Later, I promise."

Lia wondered if later would ever come.

Dinner, though, turned out to be much less than the ordeal she'd anticipated. There were no subtle questions about her past or attempts to ferret out her feelings for Duran, no sense from Duran's parents she fell short of their expectations for their son. Instead they talked about Noah and the upcoming transplant, Duran's newfound brothers and even Jed.

Lia was ready to admit the evening was going well when, halfway through dessert, her cell phone buzzed. Excusing herself, she went outside to take the call, coming back a few minutes later.

She shook her head at Duran when he stood up to pull out her chair. "I'm sorry, that was my stepmother. I have to go home. There's an emergency."

Chapter Fifteen

Lia opened her door to Duran and he immediately saw the tension and tiredness in her eyes and the taut lines of her neck and shoulders. She'd changed into the drawstring shorts and camisole top he remembered from their nights in the Pinwa village. It stirred desires, both complex and base, reminding him it was late evening and he'd come alone.

"Duran—" Her voice lifted in a note of surprise. "Is something wrong?"

"I was going to ask you that. I had my parents pick up Noah and take him back to the ranch. They're staying with him until I get back. After that call at dinner, I wanted to make sure everything was okay."

Her smile was little more than a brief, humorless lift of her mouth. "No, everything is a damn mess, but it isn't unexpected either. Do you want to come in?" she offered, already standing aside. "Nina's sleeping. Finally."

"Nina?" he asked as he accepted her invitation and she closed the door behind him.

"My sister."

She led him into a living room that held the bare essentials of furniture. Yet each piece had obviously been chosen with care, the colors and patterns in warm shades of autumn. He turned down her offer of a drink and took a seat next to her on the couch.

Pushing her hands through her hair, she leaned her head back against the cushions, closed her eyes and sighed. "I'm sorry I had to leave in the middle of dinner. But when Madelyn called, it was basically to tell me she was dropping Nina on my doorstep. I didn't trust her not to just dump Nina and leave. Nina's four," she explained. "And Madelyn acts like a child sometimes."

"And Madelyn is—"

"My latest stepmother. Although it's hard to think of someone six years younger than me as a stepmother. She and my father apparently had the fight of the decade when Madelyn told him she was pregnant again and then he walked out and Madelyn had a meltdown. She was almost hysterical when she called and practically begged me to take Nina. My father made it clear he didn't want any more children after Nina. But Madelyn likes being Mrs. Dr. Walter Kerrigan and I guess she thought another baby would earn her the title for life. His three ex-wives should have told her the odds of that happening."

She shifted to look at him, her expression hesitant. "I hated having to leave like that," she said. "But I couldn't just turn my back on Nina. Madelyn wasn't in any shape to take care of her. She can't take care of herself when she gets like this. And my dad apparently refused to come and get Nina. She doesn't have anybody else right now." The fabric of the pillow next to her suddenly seemed to capture her attention. "My family isn't like yours. Our response to a crisis is to distance ourselves from it as quickly as possible. God forbid any of us should support the others."

"Except for you," Duran said quietly. He reached out and took her hand, lacing their fingers together. "You care. Nina's lucky to have you."

A light flush stained Lia's cheeks, but before she could respond, the door behind them edged open and a little girl, dark hair mussed and rubbing sleepily at her eyes, took a faltering step into the living room.

Lia was quickly on her feet and at the child's side, putting an arm around her. "What's the matter, sweetie?"

"I want Mommy. Where's Mommy?"

"Mommy will be back soon," Lia soothed.

Nina's lower lip trembled. "I wanna go home. *When* is Mommy coming?"

"In a little while, I promise." She hugged Nina and over the child's shoulder, her eyes squeezed tightly shut, her lips pressed tight. When she pulled back, she made an effort to smile. "Where's your kitty? I'll bet he needs a hug, too."

"I can't find kitty," Nina said, her mouth screwed up in a frown.

"Oh, I'm sure he's just hiding under the blankets. Come on, we'll go and find him." With an apologetic glance at Duran, Lia led Nina back into the bedroom.

For a several minutes, Duran could hear murmurs through the half-open door and then Lia's voice, gentle and soothing, singing her sister a lullaby.

The image it evoked seemed at odds with the woman who'd been uncomfortable with the whole warm, bonded atmosphere generated by his family, both his parents and his newfound brothers. Even his parents had recognized it. Though they'd not said anything directly even after Lia left, Duran knew they were concerned he was setting himself up for another loss, another heartache, by getting involved with her.

Their unspoken doubts served to underscore his own, leaving him wondering if Lia would yet find an excuse to back out of her promise to go with him and Noah to Albuquerque. He was angry at himself for even having the thought but it stuck in his head and he couldn't rid himself of it.

Lia came out of the bedroom, carefully shutting the door, and then dropping back on the couch with her arms folded tightly across her chest. "I could strangle them both," she muttered.

If she'd telegraphed tension before, now she positively radiated it. Duran slid over next to her, eased her around until her back was to him, then gently started kneading shoulders and neck. Her muscles were so tight that to start, it felt like massaging stone. "What are you going to do about Nina?" he asked.

"Keep her with me while I try to get her parents to act like adults. Madelyn's not my favorite person, but she loves Nina and Nina needs to be with at least one of her parents. My father—" She shook her head, her mouth a hard line. "He'll be too occupied with figuring how much more child support a new baby is going to cost him to worry about his daughter."

He didn't want to say it but found himself telling her, "I'll understand if this means you can't make the Albuquerque trip. It's more important you be there for Nina."

Abruptly, she pulled away from him and Duran expected her to grab the excuse. Instead she faced him, eyes narrowed. "I won't abandon Nina, but I'm pretty sure in a day or two she'll be back with Madelyn. Since you're not leaving for a week, it shouldn't be an issue. It sounds to me, though, like you're looking for a reason I should stay here."

"No, I'm not," he said, although it was more of a half-truth than he wanted to admit.

"But—?"

"But you're right, my family's different than yours and they're going to be around in Albuquerque, too. I don't want to put you in another situation where you're going to feel uncomfortable."

"Duran, look—" She sighed. Pressing her fingers into her forehead for a moment, she looked back up and there was an uneasy mix of vulnerability and resolve in her expression. "I admit that sometimes—maybe a lot of the time—I feel like an alien around your family even when I'm with you and Noah. You've had the storybook childhood and now you've got this big, loving extended family and I had— Well, this mess with Nina is minor compared with some of the other stunts my parents have pulled over the years. I want what you've got, but I don't know how to get it and I wouldn't know how to act if I did. Maybe that's why I act so crazy sometimes because if I did get it, I'm afraid I'd screw it up."

She warded him off with a hand to his chest when Duran would have interrupted. "None of that is important. No matter what happens, I'm going with you and Noah. Okay?"

It was important, though, and he couldn't quell the doubts that her feelings for him and Noah would be stronger than her fears.

"Okay," he answered softly.

Eyeing him as if she were skeptical of his agreement, she said, "That was almost too easy."

"It doesn't always have to be hard or complicated."

"Maybe, but some days it seems like it." She rolled her shoulders back, arching with a wince. "Feels like it, too."

Without answering, he shifted to put himself behind her

again, continuing his slow massage from where he'd left off. Tense at first, she gradually began to relax, softening under the rhythmic touch of his hands.

"I'll give you an hour to stop that," she murmured.

"Only an hour?"

"How long— Oh…" It came out almost as a moan of pleasure as he worked his thumbs down between her shoulder blades. "Keep that up and I may ask for all night."

One night wouldn't be enough, and he wasn't thinking of an innocent massage. As if by his body's bidding, ignorant of his mind's warnings, he moved closer to her, brushing her hair aside and lightly pressing his lips to the warm, bare skin of her nape.

She drew in a breath and his name came out on a shuddering sigh. "Duran…"

Smoothing his hand over her shoulder and down her arm, sliding the strap of her camisole away with it, his mouth followed the same path. She reached up and curled her fingers into his hair, turning slightly so she could press a kiss against his cheek.

Duran cupped her face in one hand and brought her mouth to his. Softly caressing at first, their kiss became frankly sensual when she twisted into his arms, both her hands now around his neck and holding him to her.

With the slightest indication she wanted more, he could easily have succumbed—which made it all the more disappointing when she ended it after a few minutes by slowly easing out of his embrace. She gave him a poor attempt at a smile.

"Duran, I want—but…" She glanced at the closed door behind them. "I can't, not with Nina here."

"And I should get back to Noah." He stood up, trying to distance himself—not from her—but from his own desire to ignore what was right, and do what he so urgently wanted.

He didn't realize she'd risen until he felt her hand, gently threading into his hair, caressing against his neck. She kissed the side of his throat, rested her forehead against his collarbone. "It never seems like the right time for us," she murmured.

His body painful with a need that had gone unfulfilled for too long now, he muttered, "I'm willing to give wrong a try," and she laughed. Realizing how much like a frustrated teenager he sounded, he reluctantly smiled. "A right time does seem hard to come by, especially lately. Unfortunately, with everything going on, I don't see it getting much better any time soon."

"And that means?" she asked, but, *So, you're giving up?* is what he heard.

With a touch of his fingers to her cheek, he drew her eyes back to his. There were fear and resignation in hers. "That means it's hard and complicated. It doesn't mean it isn't worth it."

Silent for a moment, she studied him with an almost unnerving intensity. "Do you still believe it's worth it? Honestly?"

"Do you?" His hesitation in answering, throwing her question back at her, had her quickly averting her eyes and taking a step back. "Lia—" Duran caught her hand to keep her from turning away. "I'm not giving up. I just need to be sure you aren't either."

She said nothing to reassure him, only nodded. At her door, she returned his kiss with an almost desperate urgency, before breaking it off with a more subdued touch of her mouth to his.

Her only promise was to call him soon and as he left her, Duran made himself believe it.

She wasn't coming.

Sure of that now, Duran resigned himself to having to tell Noah that they'd be traveling to Albuquerque alone.

It wasn't a task he looked forward to. Noah was depending on Lia being there with them and Duran hated to start off what promised to be a long arduous journey ahead by disappointing his son.

He didn't see any way around it, though. Lia, as she'd promised, had kept in touch the last week, calling both him and Noah, often more than once a day and stopping by the ranch once to check on Noah in person. But as of yesterday afternoon, she still hadn't resolved anything with Nina and her father and stepmother. It was now nearly nine, he hadn't heard from her today at all, and he doubted she'd be able to come up with a last hour solution before tomorrow's early morning drive to the medical center.

He told himself he'd manage. He'd expected this, after all, been doubtful all along she'd be able to keep to her commitment. His parents were going to join them a few days before the actual transplant and Sawyer and Maya also would be there for the procedure. He'd have the support of his family so maybe it was better he, and especially Noah, didn't rely on Lia any more than they already had.

It all sounded sensible and yet felt anything but. The prospect of going back to being alone, handling everything with Noah alone, left him feeling emptier than he'd ever known possible.

Pushing the last of Noah's T-shirts into their suitcase, he zipped it shut. That was all of it, barring a few late additions to the carry-on, and so, ready as he'd ever be, he looked into the bedroom to assure himself Noah was still sleeping. The medication Noah had been taking prior to the transplant lowered his resistance and his energy levels so his son tired out much sooner than before. It was just as well Noah was in bed early, though, because Duran didn't want him overhearing when he called Lia.

He couldn't leave without talking to her and he wanted to do it in person. But ten minutes later, after having called her cell, her office and her apartment, he was frustrated at only having gotten her answering service and receptionist, both telling him she wasn't available.

Great. The last thing he wanted to do was resort to leaving her a message. But tomorrow he'd be faced with calling her early on the drive to Albuquerque and he wouldn't be able to talk freely.

Staring down at the cell phone in his hand, he made the decision and punched in her number again.

I appreciate you trying to work it out to go with us and I understand why you can't make it. If it were my sister, I'd do the same thing. Like you said, our timing seems to be bad. I'll call you when we get to Albuquerque. We'll miss you.

Lia jabbed off the message so hard it jarred her hand.

She'd come home after ten, tired, emotionally drained, but relieved that after hours spent talking with her father and then making the drive to Santa Fe to meet with Madelyn, Nina was now happily back home with her mother. Things were still angry and unresolved between her father and his wife and that she couldn't fix. Madelyn, though, had at least pulled herself together enough to realize she needed to put her daughter first. With the latest crisis downgraded, Lia had been looking forward to focusing on the trip to Albuquerque.

Duran's message had changed everything.

In the span of a few minutes, she went through a whole gamut of feelings, from frustrated and upset, to sorrowful and disappointed, and finally, determined that, for once in her life, she wouldn't let things die without a fight. She cared too much about Duran and Noah to watch them walk out of her life without even a whimper of protest.

Her resolve lent her a surge of energy. She didn't bother calling Duran. For too long, she'd been relying on him to take the lead in their relationship and show her the way. She'd blamed her past for her refusal to consider a future with him and consequently had given him reason to doubt they could ever be together.

All her life, she'd been standing on the edge of the leap of faith needed to truly love someone, looking down, afraid of falling. She was still afraid but not so crippled by fear that she couldn't act.

This time, she knew what she had to do.

Draining his coffee mug for the third time, Duran glanced at his watch and decided he needed to wake Noah. It was barely seven but they had a three-hour drive to Albuquerque and they needed to get started soon if they were going to be at the hospital by early afternoon.

He was headed back toward his and Noah's rooms when the front door chime, followed by a strident knocking, pulled him up short. Thinking that at this hour it had to be one of his brothers, Duran went to answer it.

Lia stood there, a bag slung over her shoulder and another at her feet.

They looked at each other. She didn't give him time to react.

"I made a promise to you and Noah and I'm not going to break it," she said firmly. "I'm going with you."

Chapter Sixteen

Lia put down the game controller with a sigh of mock exasperation. "Okay, I give up. That's the eighth time I've gotten zapped by that little blue critter." She looked over at Noah. He grinned and she laughed. "You're just too good for me."

"That's 'cause I play way more than you do. You're not *too* bad," he added, generous in his fourth consecutive victory.

"Thanks—I think. I guess that's better than being totally terrible."

Duran looked up from his laptop where he'd been editing a commercial and smiled over at them. "Noah's just going to have to give you a few more lessons."

"If I remember correctly, he beats you all the time, too," Lia teased. "I think we both need lessons."

That elicited a giggle from Noah but his glee at besting the adults was short-lived. Rubbing at his eyes, he put down his own controller and leaned back against the pillows. Lia set both controllers aside and adjusted the pillows a little lower as Noah hugged an arm around Percy.

"Getting sleepy again, buddy?" Duran asked softly, coming over to sit next to Noah. He gently stroked his son's head and Noah inched closer to rest his cheek against Duran's side.

Duran exchanged a glance with Lia. He knew, as she did, that the chemotherapy Noah had been given over the last week in preparation for the transplant was the reason he tired so easily, was the cause of the darker circles under his eyes and his unhealthy pallor. He also knew—and hated—that there was nothing he could do to make things easier for his son except stand by, wait with him, and try, as both he and she had been doing, to keep Noah's spirits up.

A nurse came in for one of Noah's periodic checks and Duran moved next to Lia, watching intently as the nurse looked at the catheter in Noah's chest. Lia slipped her hand in Duran's, squeezing lightly, and he grasped her fingers more firmly, his grip briefly tightening when Noah winced at the nurse's gentle prodding.

It had been that way, between them and with him, ever since their arrival in Albuquerque. They had found it easy, natural, to hold hands, to touch each other, as if they both needed reassurance that they were truly together in this, and that her being there with him and Noah was right.

Duran seemed to need it even more as a steadying influence. As they waited out the ten days of preparation before the transplant, he was more on edge than Lia had ever seen him. Yet at the same time he drew from her strength in a way that made her feel needed, essential maybe. The shadows under his eyes almost rivaled Noah's and she knew without him admitting it that he hadn't been sleeping well.

Right now, she was his primary support, the only one there to remind him to sleep, eat, get out of the hospital the times Noah was sleeping; to keep him grounded when his worrying got the better of his cautious optimism. She was glad to be here for him, for them both. Being here now, so bonded with Duran, she couldn't imagine how he would have gotten through this had they not met. He would have, of course, but the way he bounced every thought, question, fear, hope and idea off of her lately, she wanted to believe she meant as much to him as it seemed she did.

Duran's family called regularly—his parents at least once, often two or three times a day in between visits—and Cort, the days he was in town for classes at the university law school, had also stopped by several times. But mostly the three of them were alone together, dealing with the barrage of new challenges thrown Noah's way every day.

The nurse finished and after she'd gone, Lia and Duran moved together to Noah's bedside.

"Are you leavin'?" Noah mumbled.

"No, we're not leaving yet," Duran said softly. "You need to get some sleep, though. We'll be here when you wake up."

"Promise?" He clutched Percy more tightly, his gaze—a plea for reassurance—moving back and forth between his father and Lia.

Duran's smile wasn't quite steady. He bent and gave Noah a hug, careful of the various tubes and wires. "Promise. Now close your eyes and try to get some rest, okay?"

Noah nodded and less than ten minutes later, was deeply asleep. With a tug to Duran's arm, Lia inclined her head to the door.

"Let's go for a walk," she said when they were outside the room. She stopped his protest with quick fingers against his mouth. "He'll be asleep for at least an hour, probably more. Half an hour outside isn't breaking your promise."

There was a small garden and playground area on the hospital grounds and they found their way there, sharing a bench facing the swings and the flowers. They had the place to themselves and the late afternoon warmth seemed to mute the sounds around them.

"Only a few more days of this and then they'll be able to do the transplant," Lia ventured after the silence stretched between them for several minutes.

"And then we start the waiting all over again. You'd think I'd be good at it by now." With a huff of humorless laughter, Duran jerked to his feet, dragging his hands over his hair.

"No parent who loves his child is good at this."

He turned to her. "I haven't told you, but I'm glad you're here with me. Before we left Luna Hermosa, I'm sorry, but I didn't think you'd end up coming with us."

"It's okay," she hurriedly interrupted. "For a while, I didn't trust myself to follow through, either. But I'm glad I came."

"I don't know what I would have done without you."

"You'd have done what you've always done, been there for Noah."

"I guess. It doesn't feel that way any more though. When I have a thought or worry, or when I just want to rest and talk about nothing, you're the one person I think of turning to. I can't do that with anyone else."

"Your family—"

"It's not the same. I've tried not to worry my parents any more than necessary. And anyone else—no one understands like you do." He smiled a little. "Or maybe it's just nobody else puts up with me like you do."

"I'm sure that's it," Lia said, returning his smile. "But it's mutual."

The brief lightening of his expression dimmed and he let out a long breath. "I just keep wondering if there's something else we should be doing."

The *we* made them a team and was a commitment in itself. Maybe it was temporary, fated only to last as long as the current crisis in his life. But hearing it left Lia high on hope that, this time, it could last for both of them.

"We're doing all we can right now, just being with him," she said. "There's nothing else we can do except let the doctors do their job."

"I know, but it doesn't feel like enough. It never does." Wincing, Duran pressed two fingers between his eyes. "I should be making plans. There's all the school Noah's missing. We had been keeping up with assignments at home, but lately he's just too exhausted. Also, I need to get this new project started, and I've got to think seriously about making the move to New Mexico I talked about because Noah's going to have to be near the hospital for a while to come. Then I need to—"

"Okay, stop." She held up her hands. "Your brain is going to explode if you keep this up." With pursed lips, she looked around them and then grabbed his arm and started pulling him toward the swings.

"Lia, I don't think—"

"Good. Not thinking is good." She grabbed the nearest swing and pushed it toward him. "This one's yours."

She ignored his reluctance and made him do it all, swings, slide, seesaw, and several trips on the merry-go-round, until they were both dizzy and collapsed on the grassy area, laughing at each other.

Still smiling, Duran lightly skimmed his fingertips over her face, his eyes more expressive of his feelings than any words could have been. He bent closer then and kissed her, long and tenderly, until she was warm and dizzy in a very different way, and everything seemed just a little bit easier.

It was well past eight when they finally left the hospital for the night, Noah lulled to sleep again by their assurances that keeping to the routine they'd established, they'd be back in time for tomorrow's breakfast.

As he made the turn into their hotel parking lot, Duran glanced at her and said, "I was thinking of ordering takeout and eating in tonight."

"That's fine." She tried to quell a surge of disappointment that he'd decided to forgo their habit of eating dinner together before they returned to their separate rooms.

Determined not to overanalyze his motives or read more into them than he intended, and already turning plans over in her mind for salad and a movie, and maybe afterward, a late night call to Nova, she nearly missed him questioning, "Is Thai okay?"

It took her a moment to process that he was asking her to dinner in his room and only when his mouth twitched in an effort to hold back a smile did she realize she'd probably been staring stupidly without answering.

"Thai's good," she said with an attempt at casual that didn't come off very well. She knew her face had to be an unlovely shade of pink right now. Blessedly, he didn't comment.

She expected at least some awkwardness about the intimacy of being alone with him in his hotel room at night. But Duran had a long-term suite with a separate bedroom so there was no bed in plain sight to suggest other activities besides dinner and conversation. That relaxed her and he seemed to take his cue from her, talking about when his parents and Sawyer and Maya would be coming, and Eliana's promise to bring Sammy for a visit on the weekend, she in turn telling him a little more about Nina and the latest between her father and Madelyn.

"I got an e-mail from Ry today," he threw out when they were partway through dinner. "He was asking about Noah."

"You sound surprised."

"I am. He didn't seem all that enthusiastic about staying in touch even though we agreed we would. I've been keeping him updated on what's been going on with Noah and the family but this is only the second time I've gotten anything back from him." He toyed with the remains of his curry. "I'm not sure I'd call the first time an actual reply, more like two short lines."

"Do you think he wants to meet your family?" she asked.

"I don't think Ry wants a family period," Duran answered bluntly. "This whole business seems to be an intrusion into his life he'd rather be without. I get the impression he's used to being alone and that he likes it that way."

Lia wondered but kept quiet because the only things she knew for certain about Ry Kincaid were what Duran had told her. "How do you feel about that? I mean, you're twins. If nothing else, I'd think he'd want to get to know you better because of that."

"I haven't really thought about it. It's been enough trying to get used to all the family here that I've suddenly acquired. I'd like to get to know him since we never had the chance to grow up together. And the whole twin thing—" He shook his head. "But I'm not sure with Ry that's ever going to happen."

"I'm sorry about that," she said, unable to keep a note of wistful sadness from coloring her reply. "I've always regretted not knowing my own brothers and sisters better. It just never happened."

"But it could. Look at me. The circumstances are different, but I never knew any of my brothers even existed and now, with the exception of Ry, we're calling each other family."

Lia picked at her own food to avoid looking at him and then put the half-empty carton on the low table in front of them. "It's not quite the same. I don't think I'd get as warm a welcome as you did if I decided to show up on their doorsteps. Their reaction would probably be more like Ry's. I'd be intruding into their lives." Quiet for a moment, she raised her eyes to his and said, "I should try. I haven't tried because I always expected the worst. But the worst isn't always what happens. Sometimes things work out better than you ever expected."

"Much better," he agreed. The husky note in his voice was as palatable as a caress against her bared skin.

Temptation stronger than common sense, she suddenly leaned into him and kissed him.

The corner of his mouth lifted. "What was that for?"

"Thank you," she said, "for letting me come with you and Noah. For not giving up on me."

She wanted to tell him so much more, that she'd fallen in love with him, that he was the man who'd made her believe it was possible. But admitting it aloud might shatter her fragile hopes and she didn't want to lose them just yet.

"I should be the one thanking you."

Lia rolled her eyes. "Not again."

"Okay, then," Duran said with a laugh, "how about, you're welcome."

"Better."

Setting aside the rest of his own dinner, he rolled his neck and shoulders, wincing slightly.

"You need to get some sleep yourself," she said, watching him as he shifted to face her.

"So you've been telling me, and I have been."

"I'm not counting those naps you take in the hospital room chair when you think Noah and I aren't looking. Let me help you clean this up and then I'll go so you can get some real rest."

She started to get up but Duran caught her hand, stopping her. "Leave it. You don't need to run off just yet."

"I wasn't running," she said, thinking of the other times he'd accused her of running away from him, from her feelings. "This is different."

"I know it is."

They looked at each other, confirming wordlessly what they both wanted. In the next moment, they were in each other's arms, kissing with a passionate intensity that felt like a release of all the emotions they'd denied and tried to explain away or avoid the last months.

She encouraged him, drawing him down, when he eased her back against the arm of the couch, anticipating his hands and mouth on her body with an urgency that matched her desire to touch him in return. He didn't disappoint her, kissing her neck, her throat, as he worked free the buttons of her shirt while she pushed up his.

It felt like they'd waited a lifetime to love each other and it made Lia greedy for everything he would give her, to give him anything he wanted.

At the urging of her hands, he yanked off his T-shirt and tossed it aside. Yet he gave her scant time to explore, pulling open her shirt, freeing the front clasp of her bra.

"Duran…" she breathed his name as he slid his hands over her breasts, the intimate caress driving every thought from her mind except the desire to be even closer.

"You don't know how many times I've thought about this," he said, his voice rough with need.

"Love me," she whispered against his mouth.

"I do."

He kissed her deeply, robbing her of the ability to reply, and she could only kiss him back, hoping he could hear her heart speak through her touch. *I love you, too.*

Leaning back enough to look into her eyes, he said softly, "I want to make love with you. But if it's not what you want—"

She answered him with a kiss, intimate and sensual, and expressing desires long held and yet unfulfilled. There was no reason to wonder if being with Duran was right. Here and now, all the reasons she'd conjured for not loving him seemed petty and insignificant compared to the powerful surge of feeling evoked by his touch. At once achingly tender and passionate, it left in its wake desire and need and an unshakable certainly they belonged together.

He seemed to share her impatience with any of the preliminaries of small talk or teasing to build the expectancy. She didn't protest when, with obvious reluctance, he pulled out of their embrace, took her hands in his and led her to the bedroom. She wanted everything he did.

The single light cast a soft glow, and he stopped to look at her, searching her eyes, an expression of wonder in his, as if he couldn't believe she was there. He reached out a hand and touched her cheek, so gently it was like a whisper against her skin.

"I want to take this slowly," he said, his voice low and rough. "I don't know if I can." He shook his head as if to clear it. "You…overwhelm me."

He was left without words and she understood. They didn't need them. Stepping toward him she wrapped her arms around his neck, while at the same time he pulled her against the length of his body and met her in an intimate kiss.

The way he made her feel—hot and aching, almost desperate to get closer to him—urged her to hurry, to take and offer everything possible. Fingers trembling, she pushed at the button of his jeans, the task becoming almost impossible when he began doing things with his teeth and tongue to the side of her neck and the sensitive spot just below her ear, igniting every nerve in her body.

Her moan, half frustration, half pleasure, drew a husky laugh from him. "Are you always this impatient?"

"You were the one who said you couldn't wait," she reminded him. Splaying her hands over his chest, reveling in the touch of skin to skin, she tempted him to forget any ideas of slow and easy. She leaned in to kiss the hollow of his throat, along his collarbone, his shoulder where the tattooed *kanji* reminded her of what had brought them here, to a place where only their feelings for each other mattered.

Faith. Courage. Love.

"I've, ah…Lia—" Her fingers trailing over his ribs and lower, to skim against his arousal, pulled a groan from him and shook the resolve in his voice.

He took her face in his hands and she could see everything in his eyes—desire, need and an emotion deeper and more affecting than both. "You're worth waiting for. I want it to be—perfect." He punctuated the last word with a kiss, slowly working his mouth and tongue around hers, inflaming the anticipation in them both.

Clothing became a hindrance when all she wanted against her body was him. Duran complied by undressing her, but without hurry, as if he was intent on using every sense to memorize her.

He explored every area he bared with his hands and mouth with a thoroughness that left her pliant, yielding to sensation, willfully abandoning reason. Her shirt and bra quickly discarded, he dropped to his knees in front of her, sliding off her jeans and then the scrap of lace that was the last barrier to his touch, so all she wore was skin and a flush of desire.

She wanted to do the same for him; he had other ideas. Staying at her feet, he teased her, caressing her hips and thighs in languorous strokes, nuzzling kisses within inches of where she ached for him to touch her, until she was nearly wild with her need for him. She urged him up but he stubbornly continued his play for a few moments longer before finally giving in to her plea.

But when she expected him to finish what they'd started, he surprised her by turning her toward the bed, gently guiding her to kneel on the end so she faced the mirrored closet door.

Something seemed to go wrong with her breathing as she watched the reflection in the mirror: him stripping off the rest of his clothes, moving behind her, his body hard and hot where it brushed hers. He ran his tongue up the length of her spine and she shuddered, arching into him, encouraging him to mold her body to his. His name escaped her lips on a breath of longing.

"If anyone interrupts now," she murmured, "I'll have to kill them."

Duran laughed softly, seductively. Sliding his hands up to her breasts, his caresses becoming more intimate, he brushed a lingering kiss on her shoulder. "No interruptions. I promise."

Seeing their image in the glass intensified the feeling everywhere he touched her. She scarcely recognized the woman reflected there—the wanton picture she made with her arms raised to cradle his dark head against her fair skin, pliant to his desires and hers.

Their eyes met in the mirror. As if the erotic picture of her in his arms finally broke his patience, Duran suddenly shifted to lay her back on the bed, following her down. He kissed her passionately, hungrily, and she returned the same, certain she was branded by his touch, his kiss, so that every other sensation after this would be a poor shadow of this intoxicating feeling.

Again, he made them both wait, loving her with his mouth and hands until he'd coaxed her to the first peak and she was left trembling in his arms. Only then did he gather her close and kiss her deeply as she fisted her hands in his hair, wrapped her legs around his hips and welcomed him inside her.

They came back to her then, as whispers and memories, those three words that were the foundation of everything he believed. *Faith. Courage. Love.*

And as he made love to her, with passion and tenderness— and love—she realized in that moment she believed, too.

He had never loved like this before, and if there were memories of other lovers he'd once had, they were gone, burned away in the single instant he and Lia joined together, replaced with only her.

For all his fantasizing, all the nights alone, imagining how she would feel beneath his hands, the taste of her, he wasn't prepared for the reality of having her here in his bed. Convinced he could keep in control, he was totally unprepared when she so easily took it away. In the end he had lost it all, giving in to that temporary madness until they were both sated and spent.

She lay half draped over him now, her skin damp and her hair tangled, the thrum of her pulse under his fingers only beginning to slow.

If he was supposed to feel any regret, he couldn't manage to dredge any up. Beyond a deep satisfaction, he could only think that making love with her had proved what he'd known for a long time now, that his feelings for her were binding and irrevocable.

Stirring sleepily, she ran her fingers over his chest, lingering on his tattoo. "Disappointed?" she asked.

The question was so absurd that for a moment he wondered if she was serious. He slipped his fingers under her chin and tilted her face up to look at him. "At what? That we didn't do this sooner?"

"There's that, I suppose," she said lightly. "You were just so quiet, I wondered."

"You left me incoherent."

She rolled her eyes. "I seriously doubt that."

"Don't. I don't want you to have doubts anymore." Duran shifted to his side so they were face-to-face. Gently he brushed an errant strand of hair from her cheek, smiling as she briefly closed her eyes and pressed into his touch. "Lia—" She looked at him and he kissed her softly and murmured huskily, "I love you."

Her eyes widened and she went very still.

"I have for a long time. I called it a lot of things and tried to pretend it would go away. But it didn't. It hasn't. I love you."

"Duran...I—" She stopped, ran her tongue over her lips. "I want to—" Shaking her head, she looked away, but not before he saw the glint of tears.

"It's all right," he said, cupping her cheek to turn her back to him. "You don't have to say anything. They're only words, and I know. I don't need to hear them."

"You deserve them, though. But this time I'm afraid." There was bitterness in her voice and he recognized that it was turned against herself. "I've lost everyone I've ever said them to. I don't want to lose you."

"You won't." He pulled her close, stroking her hair, her back. "I love you and I know you love me, too. That's enough for now."

He kissed her, hard and passionately, affirming it to himself, determined to convince her. She held him tightly and kissed him back, her hands restless on his body, rekindling his desire, crowding out all thoughts except ones of loving her again.

And for the length of the night, there were no doubts or fears, only them.

Chapter Seventeen

They held vigil in the small space near Noah's room, and of all the countless hours leading up to this day, Duran was sure these were the longest.

The transplant team was prepping Noah for the procedure that could save his life and in a little over an hour, it would be over—and just beginning.

"It won't be long now," Lia said quietly. Her fingers laced with his, she squeezed gently, telling Duran through her touch she understood.

He knew she did. Of all of them there waiting with him—his parents, Sawyer and Maya—she was the one he needed there the most.

"And then we start the waiting again," he said.

"Yes, but after the transplant is done, the waiting won't be as long and hopefully the result will be Noah gets better.

Duran tried to hold on to his faith that that would happen,

tried to set aside the worries about the transplant itself that he knew were real. Lia and the transplant doctor had warned him that at best, Noah might experience minor pain and chills; at worst, hives, chest pain, fever—which could make him far more susceptible to infections and excessive bleeding after the graft. "I need to be in there with him."

Lia's grip on his hand tightened. "I know."

"I still can't believe they're not taking him into an operating room," Eliza said from her seat next to her husband. Only Duran and Lia had stayed standing, Duran too restless to sit. "It's more sterile there and there's all that equipment for emergencies."

"Noah is actually much better off in his room," Lia said soothingly. "What he's having done is pretty simple, like a blood transfusion. Sawyer made his donation a couple of days ago, so the whole procedure will go pretty quickly. And Noah's used to his room. He'll be more comfortable there with familiar things around him."

"Once this is done, we've got what? A week or two before we know it worked?" Sawyer asked.

"If it works—" Duran inwardly winced at the gentle stress Lia put on the *if* "—then, yes, it'll be a couple of weeks before the new bone-marrow cells start multiplying and making blood."

"After all this, I can't believe it won't work," Eliza said. She dabbed at her eyes with a crumpled handkerchief, managing a weak smile when her husband patted her hand.

"We thank God Duran found you in time, Sawyer," Luke said. "It's a miracle he ended up having so much family and that one of you was a match for Noah."

At last, Lia thought, the waiting would come to an end.

"We're just glad Duran came looking for us," Sawyer told him.

"And we're glad to have him and Noah in our family,

too," Maya added. "You've both been so wonderful about accepting that."

Eliza shook her head. "How could we not? You've done so much for our son and Noah." Her gaze encompassed all of them, lingering seconds on Lia and Duran and their clasped hands. "All of you."

Feeling Lia shift at his side, Duran could almost hear her wondering if their display of closeness in front of his parents and his brother and the message it gave his family was what he wanted. No one knew they were lovers but it was obvious they were more than friends—that Lia wasn't simply the pediatrician who'd taken a caring interest in Noah.

"Everyone's been great but if it hadn't been for Lia, Noah would have had a lot harder a time," he said, making it clear to her and everyone else how important she'd become to him. "She's been so terrific with him, everyone assumed at first she was his mother."

It amazed him how easily he could imagine her in that role, the mother that his son had never had—and the lover, partner and friend he had once been certain he'd never have in his life again.

Before he had come to Luna Hermosa, his belief that it would never happen couldn't have been shaken.

Now, with Lia at his side, his hope that it could happen had been renewed.

"Thanks, I needed this." Taking the cup of fragrant herbal tea from Maya, Lia took a small sip, savoring both the aroma and flavor of the lavender and primrose blend. "I've been overdosing on caffeine lately."

"I'm not surprised," Maya said.

Maya had been the one to suggest Lia accompany her to the cafeteria so Maya could find hot water for the organic brew she favored and they could bring back coffee for the rest of the waiting-room party. Lia suspected Maya, with her fine-tuned empathy, had thought Lia needed a brief reprieve, and maybe she had—at least from the speculative looks she and Duran kept getting from his parents.

Insisting Lia have a cup of tea with her before they went back to the waiting room, Maya had found them a corner table on an outside patio away from the hustle and bustle of the busy cafeteria. "Duran's parents are nice, aren't they?" she commented lightly.

"They're practically perfect."

"I doubt it, but nice isn't such a bad thing."

"No, it isn't. It's just that when I compare them to my mom and dad, well, night and day is an understatement. I grew up in a circus and Duran grew up in a suburban utopia."

"And?"

"And it's a big difference, that's all." When Maya raised a skeptical brow at Lia's less-than-honest response, Lia sighed. "Okay, I confess I sometimes feel uncomfortable around them. I wonder what they'd think of me if they really knew me and my past."

"I doubt they'd care, but the only thing that matters is what Duran thinks. And feels," Maya added, slanting a glance at Lia as she stirred extra honey into her tea.

"You're not very subtle, you know." She smiled at Maya's unrepentant shrug, then looked down at her cup. "I think he loves me. He says he does," she said softly, savoring the words as a balm to her heart. "But I'm not sure he *wants* to be in love with me. He's scared I can't commit. I don't blame him."

"Lia, you can't keep comparing yourself to your parents. I mean, look at my parents. Shem and Azure aren't exactly your typical mom and dad."

It was true. The Rainbows were almost caricatures of themselves, hippies in every sense of the word. They'd never
married and with their flower power van, wild parties, bell-
bottoms and outlandish tie-dye shirts, they'd always been the
brunt of childhood jokes.

"Now contrast the way I grew up with the way Sawyer
grew up," Maya said. "His mother was and his grandparents
are the pinnacles of society here and throughout a good
portion of the state, shining examples of impeccable taste
and proper behavior. His grandparents were so appalled when
Sawyer and I decided to get married they all but offered to
buy me off *not* to marry him."

Maya reached across the table to touch Lia's hand. "All that
matters is how you and Duran feel about each other and how
you deal with your families and your pasts. You don't need
anyone else's approval. Not your parents, not his. You have
to trust in your love for each other. If you can do that, you'll
find a way around the rest of it."

"I want to believe it," Lia said, realizing she was admitting
to her friend she loved Duran in return. "It's just hard to have
faith when you're afraid of failing."

"I know. Just think about it, okay?" When Lia nodded,
Maya gave her hand a final pat and then glanced at her watch.
"We'd better get back to our men and check on Noah."

As they rose from the table and gathered up their cups,
Maya impulsively hugged Lia. "Give yourself a chance. I did
it and you can too. It took a lot of courage and it was terrify-
ing at first. Especially with the Morente high court judging
my every move. But look at Sawyer and me now. Trust me,
it's worth the risk."

Lia hugged her back. "I believe you."

* * *

It was over, and Duran had all the reassurances the doctors could give that the transplant procedure had gone well, giving Noah his chance at a regular, normal life.

A regular, normal life… The image of that cracked when he walked into his son's room and saw Noah lying there, pale and unmoving. As many times as he'd seen Noah hooked up to tubes, needles stuck in his arms, hands and chest, every time he saw him like this it wrenched his heart again. He stopped in the doorway and gripped Lia's hand hard.

"Don't let all of this discourage you," she said quietly. "He's weak from today and from the chemo he had in prep, but before you know it he'll be beating you in bike races."

Taking a deep breath, Duran led them both to Noah's bedside. He bent and brushed lank strands of hair from his son's brow. Lia tucked Percy a little closer.

"Hey buddy, you're a champ, you know that?" Duran said, forcing a smile.

Sleepily, Noah's eyes opened a sliver and he offered the barest hint of a smile back. The lump in Duran's throat got a size larger.

At his side, Lia's mouth curved reassuringly. "You did great, Noah," she whispered, leaning over him to touch her lips to his cheek. "Just rest and dream about that new bike of yours. When you're better you're gonna have to race me up that trail."

Noah, with the barest of nods, drifted off to sleep again and they sat on the edge of his bed in silence side by side, hand in hand until a nurse came in and reminded them the others were wanting to hear news about Noah.

Reluctantly they each kissed Noah, Lia snuggled his blanket around him while Duran fluffed his pillow, then they turned to leave.

Duran took her hand, but suddenly, overcome with a need as fierce as any he'd ever known to be closer to her, to pour out all the past days of fear and uncertainty, of gratefulness to her, of self-loathing for his doubts and questions, and to, in turn, help her bear her pain, her angst, her regrets and longings, Duran reached for Lia and pulled her hard against him, engulfing her in his arms, burying his face in her neck.

She matched his fervor, returning the embrace with equal passion, holding on to him as he clung to her, in a desperate exchange, giving and taking of strength, hope, promise and— he dared to believe—love.

"We're leaving." Lia spoke quietly, with her hand lightly gripping Duran's forearm, telegraphing her intent to succeed where his parents and brothers had failed.

Duran, looking down at his sleeping son, shook his head. "I can't."

"Yes, you can. You need to, for both your sakes."

They had both stayed the first night after the transplant, and Duran insisted on being there the night after as well, rarely leaving Noah's bedside. Tonight, though, he'd gotten the speech from his parents, Sawyer, Cort and even Noah's doctor about how he needed a break.

Logically, he knew it was true. But he was too used to dealing alone with the successive challenges and setbacks in Noah's life. He didn't trust any of them to know what was best for his son.

In the face of his stubborn refusal they had given up. All except Lia.

"Noah is doing fine," she repeated. "I've checked him myself. He's going to sleep all night, and you can be back in the morning before he wakes up. You're not doing him any good being dead on your feet."

He hesitated then said, "I'm afraid." He would never have admitted it to anyone else but he suspected she'd known it all along. She was the only one he felt comfortable sharing his vulnerabilities with because she was vulnerable, too, broken in ways he could understand. In a way they were alike in their fear of losing the people they loved. And that made her the only person to whom he could confess his reasons for sticking so close to Noah. "All I can think about are the things that could go wrong if I'm not here. I know it's stupid—"

"It's not stupid," she said softly. Gently, she cupped his face with her hand, turning him to face her. "I understand, believe me. But you need to take care of yourself, too. Noah is in very good hands for the night."

As if she anticipated his compliance, she bent and kissed Noah's forehead, lightly rubbing the back of her hand against his cheek before looking expectantly at Duran.

"Lia—"

"Don't make me call Cort," she warned in a tone that sounded serious. "He used to be a cop and I know he's more than up to the job of getting you out of here."

Her resolve, but more her understanding, won his reluctant agreement. He kissed his son and then made himself quickly turn and walk out the door before he could change his mind.

Lia drove them back to the hotel and he automatically headed for his room, not thinking beyond getting inside and some vague idea of dinner. He'd located his key card and was poised to unlock the door when he realized Lia had stopped a few feet away. She looked uncertain, of him or herself, he couldn't tell.

"Do you want me to stay?"

"You have to ask?" He didn't know why she still had her own room, except for the hassle of moving all her stuff into his suite.

"I thought, after everything, you might sleep better without me. I don't want you to think that I expect—" A light flush climbed into her face. Then she shook her head, smiling at herself. "Okay, rescue me here before I say anything dumber than that."

"It's not dumb. Believe me, I understand it." He reached for her, and she went willingly into his arms, holding him as tightly as he held her, the embrace speaking volumes about need but without the now familiar edge of desire. "Stay with me," he murmured, his cheek pressed to her hair. "I need you, Lia."

Any hesitation in her vanished as if it had never been. "I need you, too," she echoed, and, taking his hand, she walked with him into the room.

Tired and drained by the days of worrying and waiting, they settled on leftovers for dinner. There was no room service at their extended-stay hotel but Duran had a small kitchen and had enough in his fridge to put together an easy meal. Afterward, he sat on the couch with her in his arms, her back to his chest.

"I'm going to miss this," she said, and there was a wistfulness in her voice that made him tighten his embrace.

"What?" he teased gently. "Living part-time out of a hospital room, the bad coffee and takeout for dinner most nights?"

"None of the above." She tilted her head back to look at him. "I meant this, being together. Knowing that no matter what happens we'll be there for each other."

"Why does that have to change?"

"You know I've got to leave Sunday. I can't afford any more time away. I've already had a couple of emergencies that have been hard to deal with long-distance."

"That doesn't answer my question." Shifting so they faced

each other, Duran brushed an errant strand of hair from her cheek. "I know you have to go back and that it's going to be crazy for a while, with you there and us here. But Noah isn't going to be in the hospital forever. Three weeks, a month, and we'll be out of here."

"And then what?"

The question momentarily stymied him. "I don't know," he admitted. "I haven't thought that far ahead. I'm going to have to make a lot of decisions very soon, but frankly, I haven't been able to think past the next hour."

"That's not what I meant." She sat up a little straighter, hugging her arms around her knees, avoiding meeting his eyes. "I know you have to decide where you and Noah are going to live, and about a thousand other details. I meant, what do we do? If you come back to Luna Hermosa, do we keep seeing each other—personally, I mean?"

"Sweetheart, we've been doing a lot more than *seeing* each other." Seeing her light flush, he drew her back into his arms. "That's one thing I don't have to think about. I want us to stay together, all three of us. I hope that's what you want, too."

Her response was to twist around and take his face in her hands, searching his eyes before softly kissing him, the caress less sensual than tender.

Later, she wore his T-shirt and he stripped off his jeans, slipping into bed with her and gathering her close, his arms around her and her head against his chest. It wasn't entirely innocent, but it was a comfort, a silent communion of heart and soul that went deeper than physical intimacy.

They didn't talk, and after a little while, Lia's breathing evened and slowed and he lifted his head to see she'd fallen asleep. Very gently, lest he disturb her, Duran brushed his fingers against her face, fancifully imagining he was imprinting the shapes and lines of her features onto his skin—a memory to hold in his heart.

It was a long time before he joined her in dreaming; a long time before he was ready to relinquish the awe of loving her even to sleep.

"I don't want you to go!" Noah's protest was almost a wail. It had only been four days since the transplant and he continued to be sick and overly tired and to cling to Duran and Lia.

Her head told her once Noah started feeling better his tearful misery every time she and Duran were out of sight for even a few minutes would pass. Knowing that logically didn't ease the guilt or stop her from feeling a little teary herself when she tried to explain her reasons for having to return to Luna Hermosa tomorrow morning to a very unhappy little boy.

"I'll be back to visit," she said, reaching out from where she sat on the edge of Noah's bed to rub her knuckles against his cheek. "But you can't get out of here just yet and I have to go back to my job."

"You can do your job here. Dad does."

"Your dad's and my jobs are a lot different. Your dad can take his office with him, I can't. I'd have a hard time fitting a whole hospital in my purse." Noah's miserable expression didn't budge.

"Noah, we talked about this," Duran said gently from where he perched on the opposite side of the bed. "Lia isn't leaving forever, but I told you she wouldn't be able to stay the whole time."

"You'll have lots of people to keep you company," Lia tried reassuring him. "Your dad's always here, your uncle Cort and your grandparents visit all the time, and Sammy is coming again on Saturday."

"I want you!" Careless of the array of tubes and wires, Noah flung himself at Lia, clutching her tightly.

She encircled him in a close hug, her cheek against his dark mop of hair, and swallowed hard against the tightness in her throat. "Oh, sweetheart, I want to be with you, too," she said. "I just can't right now."

She couldn't quite keep her voice steady. Duran came around the bed to stand beside her, putting his arm around her shoulders. There was nothing he could say but she appreciated the contact and his silent support.

Finally, loosening her hold enough to look at Noah, she forced a smile. "You'll be out of here soon and things will be different, you'll see." She kissed his cheek, brushed the tangled hair back from his forehead. "I *will* be back, I promise. Okay?"

Noah, lower lip trembling, nodded reluctantly.

Lia couldn't resist hugging him again. "I love you," she murmured. "I'm not going to leave you."

For a brief instant, Duran gripped her shoulder hard. She glanced at him but his attention was fixed on Noah and after a moment, she too, focused on reassuring Noah once again that she wasn't abandoning him.

She and Duran stayed a little longer, until it was past visiting hours and Noah's bedtime and then stretched it out another fifteen minutes to convince themselves Noah was fast asleep.

It wasn't until much later, in the darkest hours of the night, when she was curled in Duran's arms, watching him sleep, that she realized she'd said to his son the words Duran had wanted to hear her say to him. It bothered her she hadn't yet. And despite what he'd said, she suspected from his reaction it bothered him.

Very softly, so not to wake him, she stretched up and

brushed her mouth against his. "I love you, Duran," she whispered, testing the sound and the feel of the words from her lips. He stirred, pulling her closer even in sleep as if affirming what both of them had known for a long time.

She smiled, laid her head back against his chest, silently promising them both, *I'm not going to leave you.*

Chapter Eighteen

"Daddy, you almost forgot Percy." Noah plucked his favorite stuffed friend out from under the corner of the hospital blanket. Duran had been combing the room his son had called home for over a month inch by inch in search of blocks, miniature cars and trucks, CDs and DVDs, books and stuffed toys.

"Sorry, buddy, I guess he got buried in my search."

Hopping up on a chair, Noah hugged his pal, his feet kicking air beneath him. "I can't wait to get out of here. When will Dr. Kerrigan get here?"

"Tonight. She's driving down after work to help us move back to the ranch."

Moving, Lia, their future, his new documentary, Noah's recovery, all of those thoughts had stolen Duran's sleep for the past week. Now that Noah had stabilized enough to go home, Duran had to decide where home would be.

Los Angeles wasn't an option, as Noah needed to stay fairly close to the transplant center for at least six months, maybe longer. Besides, Duran had just gotten the necessary legalities settled to start on his film about Rafe's tribe, so he'd have to live nearby to produce that.

And then there was Lia.

He pushed another toy into Noah's already overstuffed backpack. The last time she'd come to visit several days ago, things had been so good between them he felt certain he was ready to stay in Luna Hermosa, with her.

Yet her inability to tell him how she felt bred doubts and tested his trust. He reminded himself she'd certainly shown him and Noah how much she loved them both. So why couldn't she admit as much? Did it matter? Should it?

"Can we go now?" Noah asked.

Duran looked over at his son, amazed at the recent transformation. His cheeks were beginning to show some color again, his smile came more easily and more often and he was restless and eager to do things, to play, talking constantly about going biking on the trail again with Lia.

I'm gonna to beat Dr. Kerrigan up the hill, he'd promised, laughing mischievously as he explained his strategy to fool her into thinking he was still weak.

The truth was he wasn't well yet, had a long way to go to full recovery. But the transplant had taken, his bone marrow cells were reproducing successfully and the doctors were optimistic. Each day Duran thanked God he'd come to Luna Hermosa and found Lia and his family. For without them, his son might not be tugging on his arm now, begging him to take him home.

It was then, looking at the big grin on Noah's face, he knew what he had to do.

Home was Lia: flaws, fears, past and all. He'd wanted

guarantees; she couldn't give them to him. But she had given him much more, all she had to give, wholly and selflessly to him and to Noah, and it had been enough, more than enough to fill their hearts and lives.

Maybe she wasn't a woman he would once have imagined himself being with. Yet she had become the only woman he could imagine loving.

"Okay, that's the last of it," he said tossing Noah's pack over one shoulder and lifting Noah into his arms. "We are outta here."

Noah hugged his neck and Duran caught his smile, his son's happiness infectious, dispelling the shadows and lighting the way to the future.

"Mom, I'm sorry, but I don't know what to tell you."

Exasperated with trying to convince her mother to try couples' counseling one more time for her latest failing relationship, Lia handed her little sister another piece of the puzzle they were working on. "I'm babysitting Nina today while Dad and Madelyn are at the mediator for their divorce. And I'm trying to pack to drive back down to Albuquerque to help Noah and Duran move out of the hospital. This really isn't a good time for us to get into yours and Emilio's sex life."

"Well, fine, then, you seem to have time for everyone but your mother."

"Mom, please—" Lia took a breath, counted to five. "Just give me a couple of days and I'll call and we can talk all of this through."

"I'm hungry." The little girl curled up next to Lia tugged on her shirt.

"Okay, sweetie, we'll eat lunch in a few minutes. I have to go, Mom. I'll call you next week, okay?" Ending the call and lifting Nina into her arms, she stood and headed for her kitchen. "What sounds good to you? Peanut butter? Mac 'n' cheese?"

The child wrinkled her nose, lifting strands of Lia's hair to wind in between her fingers. "Milk shake."

"Grilled cheese, then milk shake."

Before they'd finished, the doorbell interrupted and Lia was surprised to find her father on her front step. "Where's Madelyn?"

Walter, his face grim, glanced over Lia's shoulder to his newest child. "She apparently needs time to herself. I'll take Nina."

"Nina, Daddy's here. Come get your backpack," she said gently, anticipating tears. Nina knew something big was happening with her parents, but she didn't exactly know what. How well Lia remembered that feeling. How much she wanted to shield Nina from all of it, now and for the next twenty years or so. But it was already too late.

She hated the vision of Nina, all grown up, trying to forge a relationship with a wonderful man, yet unable to believe it could work long-term—unable even to tell him how much she loved him. Except in her mind's eye, she didn't see Nina, but herself.

Nina shuffled over to where Lia crouched, holding the little pink and purple pack. When she got close enough, she threw her arms around Lia's neck and sniffed. "I want to stay with you."

"It's okay, sweetie." Holding Nina close and turning the child's back to her father to hide her from her father's reaction, she said, "Daddy's going to take you somewhere fun today like the park or the zoo, aren't you, Dad?"

"I wasn't—"

"But your plans changed," Lia emphasized with a scowl. "Didn't they?"

Unused to being on the receiving end of demands, Walter stared hard at her, his body stiff. After a moment of silent battle, though, his shoulders dropped in resignation. "That's right, baby," he told Nina, "I decided to take the afternoon off so you and I could go to the zoo and see that new tiger you like so much."

"That'll be fun," Lia said to her sister as she handed both Nina and the backpack to her father.

"It's a *tigger,* Daddy, like Pooh's Tigger."

"Of course it is," Walter agreed, kissing her forehead. "How could I forget?"

When they'd left, Lia rushed to finish packing, forcing her mind away from the last few hours of dealing with her dysfunctional parents, from the last years of her life, from an existence built on quicksand. Duran and Noah were the best things ever to happen to her and she didn't want to lose them.

If anyone could convince her to stop looking down, fearing the fall, and finally and irrevocably take a leap of faith, it was Duran.

She only hoped he wouldn't give up on her before she was ready to take that step away from the past and into his life.

Duran opened the door to her and before Lia could even smile a greeting, he pushed her backpack off her shoulders and had her in his arms, his mouth on hers, kissing her the way he'd wanted for the past four days.

"Wow," she breathed, when he finally paused for air.

"Yeah?"

"Oh, yeah." And she kissed him again, matching his passion, strongly reminding him how long it had been since he'd spent a night loving her.

Another hotel guest passed by, glancing at them curiously,

and they smiled at each other before moving out of the doorway and into the room.

"I'm sorry I'm so late," Lia said. "It rained all the way down and New Mexico drivers and rain aren't a good combination."

Duran nodded. He glanced to the half-opened bedroom door, to where his son lay sleeping soundly. Leaving her briefly, he walked over to close it. "Noah's passed out. He couldn't wait to get out of the hospital, but he still doesn't have as much energy as he thinks he does."

"That'll improve, with time. From what I've seen and you've said, he seems to be getting a little better every day."

"He's doing great. So am I—now that you're here."

Again he pulled her to him and they spent the next several minutes entwined, raw need electrifying the space that separated them.

Finally she eased back slightly. "I missed you." It was a breathless whisper between kisses.

"That's not even the half of it."

"Mmm…so you missed me, too?"

She was playing with his shirt buttons, her fingers wandering lower to trace the edge of his jeans and for a moment, the question didn't register. "You have to ask?"

"I haven't heard it for almost a week. So—" Her mouth brushed his. "I wondered."

"How about now?" he murmured huskily, dragging his mouth from hers to nuzzle a particularly sensitive spot he'd discovered on her neck.

"Now I'm wondering how long Noah might be asleep."

"Not long enough for what I have in mind. But long enough to talk."

"Talk doesn't sound like a very good substitute."

"Depends on what we're talking about." At her questioning look, he took her hands in his. "Lia, I love you, you know I do." He didn't wait for her to answer. He didn't need to hear what he knew she felt. "When we go back to Luna Hermosa, I want us to go back together."

"I thought that was the plan."

"I mean *together*. As a couple, a family. I want us to move in together and make a life, the rest of our lives into one life. I want you with me and Noah not just now but always."

Lia froze. She said nothing. Stared at him as if he'd told her something impossible.

"You're the love of my life, everything I'll ever need," he vowed. "I never want to be without you again."

"Duran…" she whispered in a voice that sounded rusty, unused for days. Turning away, she pushed her hands through her hair and he noticed them tremble. When she looked back, he knew her answer.

"I want to be with you, too." She held out a hand in appeal for understanding or forgiveness, or both. "I just… I wasn't ready for you to ask. Not yet."

The heat of passion gave way to a black, cold truth, one his faith in love hadn't been able to overcome. "Do you love me?"

"Yes," she said, softly, pronouncing the word with both wonder and certainty.

"Then tell me." When she only looked at him, he pushed. "I'm not asking you to give me any promises, but I need to hear you say it. I can live with the rest of it for now, but I need to know for sure that you feel the same way."

The old look of panic flashed into her eyes and although her lips parted, nothing came out.

"You can't," Duran said flatly. Pressing his palms to his temples, he paced a few steps from her, then spun back to face her.

"I don't know how we can make this work if you don't trust me enough to tell me how you feel."

"It's not you," she said, so quietly he almost didn't catch the words. Wetting her lips, she seemed to struggle to find her voice. "I don't trust love. I want to believe this will last. But every time I've believed in love before, it was taken away. When I think about that happening with you and Noah…" She gave her head a sharp shake. "I can't breathe."

"It's not going to happen with us."

"How can you be sure?"

He couldn't, and that was their problem.

They looked at each other until the weight of their doubts and fears broke the silence and she pulled in a shaky breath. "Do you want me to go?"

"No. But do you want to stay?"

For what felt like an eternity, she said nothing.

Then she glanced to the door, and Duran knew Lia Kerrigan was running again.

She almost did it.

Almost took that step and walked away from him, back to the safety of her old defenses, which didn't allow her to love or be loved, because her fear was stronger than her faith.

He had scared her, with everything he wanted from her and everything he offered.

But what frightened her more was the possibility of losing him forever.

She thought of Nova and Maya, and how they'd found the courage to forgive the past and start over. How she—and Duran, too—could do the same, if they only believed in each other.

Looking at him now, she could see he only believed that she was leaving, running once more.

He closed his eyes for a moment and when he looked at her again, there was a bleak resignation in his face. "What do you want from me, Lia?"

"Everything."

That surprised him, left him momentarily without a reply.

Lia used the small advantage to step closer. "I want to start over. I want to take that leap of faith with you and if you won't look back, I won't look down." Mustering all the courage love could give her, she held out her hand. "Hello, I'm Lia Kerrigan."

There was an agonizing moment of hesitation in him when her heart clenched and her breath caught and then he slowly reached out and took her hand in his. "Duran Forrester."

"I love you, Duran Forrester."

She said it clearly and with certainty, looking straight into his eyes so he could read the truth and know it was forever.

"I love you, too," he said and as if he couldn't bear the distance between them anymore, pulled her into his arms, burying his face in her hair. "You don't know how much."

When he shifted to bring his mouth to hers, she met him halfway, putting all her love and passion into their kiss, receiving his in return. Finally, breathless, they moved a fraction apart, enough to smile at each other and exchange those tender, searching touches that affirmed they were truly together.

"You're staying." There was only bedrock assurance in his voice that she was.

Lia nodded. "And so are you." Reaching up, she slid her hand to his face, finding the truth of it in his eyes and the almost reverent kiss he placed against her palm.

"It took me awhile," she admitted. "It took you." Her hand slipped lower, to touch his shoulder and see in her mind's eye everything they'd found together. Faith. Courage. Love. "But I finally believe."

Epilogue

Of all the places she'd left behind and revisited again, and all the times she'd been away and come back to Luna Hermosa, until today Lia had never felt she was truly coming home.

They hadn't made any plans, no decisions for the future except to return to Rancho Piñtada; hadn't thought beyond their immediate happiness. Nothing else seemed as important as the surety that, in their hearts, she, Duran and Noah were a family and wherever they were together was home.

The big ranch house was empty when they arrived late that afternoon, the misty grayness of the lingering rain bringing the shadows of evening early. Duran flicked on lights, flooding the house with a warm glow, and the three of them filled the silence with their talk and laughter as they made their way to Duran and Noah's temporary rooms.

"Are you gonna stay?" Noah asked her after they piled the luggage in corners to sort out later.

Lia met Duran's eyes and smiled. "Oh, yes," she said, answering Noah but speaking to Duran. "For a very long time."

"How long?"

"That's something we need to talk about," Duran said. He took Lia's hand and put the other on Noah's shoulder. "How would you feel if Lia stayed with us all the time, as my wife and your mother?"

Noah's eyes widened. He looked from his father to Lia and back again. "Really?"

"Your dad and I love each other and we love you, very much," Lia said, gently touching Noah's cheek. "We want all of us to be a family."

For a moment, Noah just stared at them. Then, in a rush, he launched himself at Lia and she caught him in a hug. Duran wrapped his arms around them both, their embrace lasting until Noah wriggled free enough to look up.

"This is awesome! Are you staying now? Are we gonna live here? Do I get to call you Mom?"

"Slow down," Duran said, laughing. "We'll be living here in town, but we'll have to find our own house. You get to call Lia Mom, but she can't stay just yet. She and I have to get married first."

His eyes asked her the question and there was a touch of apology in them for, she knew, not having made the proposal with candlelight and flowers, poetic words and a ring to symbolize their commitment to each other. Yet Lia thought nothing was more perfect than this, the simple affirmation of their love, the certainty that neither a ring nor a ceremony could make it more binding.

"Yes," she pronounced softly. Leaning over, she kissed him. "Yes."

The rest of the afternoon and into the evening was spent

talking about the future and answering Noah's barrage of questions about how and when and where, and why they'd decided to wait until New Year's Eve for the wedding. She and Duran didn't want to wait, either, but they both liked the idea of beginning their life together on the cusp of the new year, starting over, as they'd promised each other, without the baggage of doubts and fears.

They had finished dinner and had just moved into the great room when the front-door chime interrupted. Duran answered it to find Rafe there, his expression grim.

"I was on my way back home and saw the lights. Sorry no one was here for the homecoming." Before Duran could respond, Rafe said, "We've been at the hospital. Jed took a fall."

Duran and Lia exchanged a glance. "It doesn't sound good."

"It's not," Rafe said bluntly. "You might want to call Ry. If he's planning on coming here, he'd best not wait too long."

Leaving the hospital room, Duran ran a hand through his hair, feeling the ache of too little sleep in his back and neck.

Cruz was waiting for him. The family had been limiting their visits to one at a time and Duran had been the last of the day. "Not your favorite place to be, I'm sure."

"To be honest, I've had enough of hospitals to last me a lifetime," Duran admitted. "But the way things are with Jed..." He left the rest unsaid.

They both knew Jed's broken hip had brought on an infection that, with his immune system already weakened by the cancer treatments, could be serious at best, deadly at worst. He'd already been hospitalized for five days and the doctors had warned them his stay could be much longer.

"Any luck in reaching Ry?" Cruz asked.

"I finally got him on his cell yesterday. But all he had to say was 'thanks for calling.' I don't know what to think."

"None of us do, but you've done everything you can." Putting a hand on Duran's shoulder, he said, "Go home. That's where I'm headed. You aren't going to resolve anything with Ry by standing around here until they kick you out."

He knew Cruz was right. Getting back to Lia and Noah was certainly preferable to hanging out in a hospital corridor, speculating on his twin brother's reasons for denying his family.

As they turned to leave, neither he nor Cruz noticed the big man in the duster and battered leather hat who had stepped into the covering dark of an alcove, waiting until the pair of them had passed. When the elevator doors closed behind Duran and Cruz, the man walked up to the nurses' station.

The woman behind the desk looked up. "Can I help you?"

"Jed Garrett. How's he doing?"

"He's stable," the nurse answered carefully. She glanced at the wall clock. "Visitor's hours are over, though. If you wanted to see him—"

"I don't."

Eyeing him with a slight frown, the nurse said, "You look— have I seen you here before? Do you know Mr. Garrett?"

"No, I don't know him." His jaw set, eyes hard, Ry Kincaid turned to leave. "I don't know him at all."

* * * * *

Celebrate 60 years of pure reading pleasure
with Harlequin®!

Step back in time and enjoy a sneak preview of an exciting
anthology from Harlequin® Historical with
THE DIAMONDS OF WELBOURNE MANOR

This compelling anthology features three stories about
the outrageous Fitzmanning sisters. Meet Annalise, who
is never at a loss for words… But that can change with
an unexpected encounter in the forest.

Available May 2009 from Harlequin® Historical.

"I'm the illegitimate daughter of notoriously scandalous parents, Mr. Milford. Candidates for my hand are unlikely to be lining up at the gates."

"Don't be so quick to discount your charms, my dear. Or the charm of your substantial dowry. Or even your brothers' influence. There are as many reasons to marry as there are marriages."

Annalise snorted. "Oh, yes. Perhaps I shall marry for dynastic reasons, or perhaps for property or influence. After all, a loveless, practical marriage worked out so well for my mother."

"Well, you've routed me on that one. I can think of no suitable rejoinder." Ned rose to his feet and extended his hand. "And since that is the case, let me be the first to wish you a long and happy spinsterhood."

Her mouth gaped open. And then she laughed.

And he froze.

This was the first time, Ned realized. The first time he'd seen her eyes light up and her mouth curl. The first time he'd witnessed her features melded together in glorious accord to produce exquisite beauty.

Unbelievable what a change came over her face. Unheard of what effect her throaty, rasping laughter had on his body. It pounded a beat upon his ear, quickly taken up by his pulse. It echoed through him, finally residing in his stirring nether regions.

So easily she did it, awakened these sensations within him—without any apparent effort at all. And she had called him potentially dangerous? Clearly the intelligent thing for him to do would be to steer clear, to leave her to the tender ministrations of Lord Peter Blackthorne.

"You were right." She smiled up at him as she took his hand and climbed to her feet. "I do feel better."

Ah, well. When had he ever chosen the intelligent path?

He did not relinquish her hand. He used it to pull her in, close enough that he could feel the warmth of her. "At the risk of repeating Lord Peter's mistake and anticipating too much— may I ask if you'll be my partner in battledore tomorrow?"

Her smiled dimmed. Her breath came a little faster. His own had gone shallow, as if he'd just run a race—and lost. He ran his gaze over the appealing lift of her brow and the curious angle of her chin. His index finger twitched.

"I should like that," she said.

His finger trembled again and he lifted it, traced the pink and tender shell of her ear, the unique sweep of her jaw. Her pulse leaped beneath her skin, triggering his own. Slowly he tilted her chin up, waiting for her to object, to step back, to slap his hand away.

She did none of those eminently sensible things. Which left him free to do the entirely impractical thing.

Baby soft, the skin of her lips. Her whole body trembled when he touched her there.

He leaned in. Her eyes closed, even as she stood straight against him, strung as tight as a bow. He pressed his mouth to hers. It was a soft kiss, sweet and chaste. And yet he was hot and hard and as ready as he'd ever been in his life.

She drew back a little. Sighed. Their breath mingled a moment before she slowly backed away.

"Oh," she breathed. Her dark eyes were full of wonder and something that looked like fear. He took a step toward her, but she only shook her head. His outstretched hand fell to his side as she turned to disappear into the wood. This was the first time, Ned realized. The first time, since he'd come to the house party at Welbourne Manor, that he'd seen her eyes light up.

* * * * *

Follow Ned and Annalise's story in May 2009 in
THE DIAMONDS OF WELBOURNE MANOR
Available May 2009 from Harlequin® Historical

Available in the series romance section,
or in the historical romance section,
wherever books are sold.

We'll be spotlighting a different series
every month throughout 2009
to celebrate our 60th anniversary.

Look for Harlequin® Historical in May!

Celebrations begin with
a sumptuous Regency house party!

Join three scandalous sisters in

THE DIAMONDS OF
WELBOURNE MANOR

Glittering, scintillating, sensual fun
by Diane Gaston, Deb Marlowe
and Amanda McCabe.

**60 years of Harlequin,
600 years of romance
in Harlequin Historical!**

You're invited to join our Tell Harlequin Reader Panel!

By joining our new reader panel you will:

- Receive Harlequin® books—they are FREE and yours to keep with no obligation to purchase anything!
- Participate in fun online surveys
- Exchange opinions and ideas with women just like you
- Have a say in our new book ideas and help us publish the best in women's fiction

In addition, you will have a chance to win great prizes and receive special gifts!
See Web site for details. Some conditions apply.
Space is limited.

To join, visit us at
www.TellHarlequin.com.

REQUEST YOUR FREE BOOKS!
2 FREE NOVELS PLUS 2 FREE GIFTS!

SPECIAL EDITION®
Life, Love and Family!

YES! Please send me 2 FREE Silhouette Special Edition® novels and my 2 FREE gifts (gifts are worth about $10). After receiving them, if I don't wish to receive any more books, I can return the shipping statement marked "cancel." If I don't cancel, I will receive 6 brand-new novels every month and be billed just $4.24 per book in the U.S. or $4.99 per book in Canada. That's a savings of at least 15% off the cover price! It's quite a bargain! Shipping and handling is just 25¢ per book*. I understand that accepting the 2 free books and gifts places me under no obligation to buy anything. I can always return a shipment and cancel at any time. Even if I never buy another book from Silhouette, the two free books and gifts are mine to keep forever.

235 SDN EEYU   335 SDN EEY6

Name _____ (PLEASE PRINT) _____

Address _____ Apt. # _____

City _____ State/Prov. _____ Zip/Postal Code _____

Signature (if under 18, a parent or guardian must sign) _____

Mail to the **Silhouette Reader Service:**
IN U.S.A.: P.O. Box 1867, Buffalo, NY 14240-1867
IN CANADA: P.O. Box 609, Fort Erie, Ontario L2A 5X3

Not valid to current subscribers of Silhouette Special Edition books.

Want to try two free books from another line?
Call 1-800-873-8635 or visit www.morefreebooks.com.

* Terms and prices subject to change without notice. Prices do not include applicable taxes. Sales tax applicable in N.Y. Canadian residents will be charged applicable provincial taxes and GST. Offer not valid in Quebec. This offer is limited to one order per household. All orders subject to approval. Credit or debit balances in a customer's account(s) may be offset by any other outstanding balance owed by or to the customer. Please allow 4 to 6 weeks for delivery. Offer available while quantities last.

Your Privacy: Silhouette is committed to protecting your privacy. Our Privacy Policy is available online at www.eHarlequin.com or upon request from the Reader Service. From time to time we make our lists of customers available to reputable third parties who may have a product or service of interest to you. If you would prefer we not share your name and address, please check here. ☐

  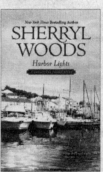

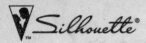
Silhouette®

COMING NEXT MONTH

Available April 28, 2009

#1969 IN CARE OF SAM BEAUDRY—Kathleen Eagle
Maggie Whiteside's nine-year-old "bad boy" had always given Sheriff Sam Beaudry the perfect excuse to flirt with the pretty single mom…until a child with an incredible secret showed up in town, bringing Sam and Maggie closer than they ever dreamed possible!

#1970 FORTUNE'S WOMAN—RaeAnne Thayne
Fortunes of Texas: Return to Red Rock
P.I. Ross Fortune had his hands full trying to exonerate his sister from a bum murder rap and look after her teenage son in the bargain. Then counselor Julie Osterman stepped up to help, and Ross found himself unable to resist the lovely social worker's appeal.

#1971 A BABY FOR THE BACHELOR—Victoria Pade
Bachelor Noah Perry never expected to meet his mate at a hardware convention; businesswoman Marti Grayson never expected to get pregnant at one! But when they reunited in Northbridge weeks later, they knew something special was building….

#1972 THE MIDWIFE'S GLASS SLIPPER—Karen Rose Smith
The Baby Experts
For Emily Diaz, hiding shameful career secrets from her boss, obstetrician Jared Madison, was bad enough. Falling in love with him as she cared for his twins only made it worse. Would she have her Cinderella moment when all could be forgiven?

#1973 RUNAWAY BRIDE RETURNS!—Christie Ridgway
Injured in a blaze, firefighter Owen Marston got a very special caretaker—runaway bride Izzy Cavaletti, who'd bolted after their quickie Vegas wedding! This time, Izzy realized she couldn't run, let alone hide, from the fire Owen lit in her heart.

#1974 THE DOCTOR'S SURPRISE FAMILY—Mary Forbes
Home to Firewood Island
When her childhood crush, military doctor Dane Rainhart, came home to Firewood Island, it was a dream come true for Kat O'Brien. But could Kat and her little boy be a cure for the heartbreak that ailed the battle-weary M.D.?